AGAINST THE GRAIN

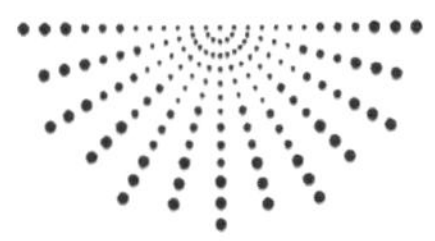

MELANIE HARDING-SHAW

CHAPTER ONE

Trinity stared around her empty flat and tried to find the energy to finish cleaning. The painkillers she'd taken were doing nothing for her headache and every time she bent over she felt as if her skin might split open from the pressure radiating inside her. She didn't want to ask for help. She was so tired of needing help.

There was a patch of broken glass near the front door where her last piece of furniture had sat until that morning. A thump sounded nearby and she turned to watch an oversized kea shove the dustpan off the breakfast bar. The alpine parrot was completely out of place in the kitchen, hundreds of kilometres and a stretch of ocean away from its native habitat.

"Saifa. Stop that."

She couldn't blame him for ignoring her flat voice as he dragged the dustpan closer with his beak. She sank down onto the cold wooden floor and reached out to touch his soft feathers.

"You know, if you were a dog I could hug you properly."

The kea's only response was to drop the dustpan and latch his beak onto her hand. Trinity cursed as the sharp point broke the skin, and then sighed in relief as she felt the burning fire of her power seeping out through the connection. A little of the pressure inside her released and her head started to clear.

I was leaving you to mope, but you can't wait that long. It's dangerous to let it build up like that. Saifa's voice sounded in her mind, the rich and sinister tone incongruous with his fussing, concerned words.

"Maybe I should just let it consume me."

Get a grip. You're hardly alone in having autoimmune conditions. They're not that bad.

"So I should spend the rest of my life running from men who smash the windows in?"

Trinity's mind flashed back to the night before, the sounds of broken glass, the flurry of feathers as Saifa changed into a Haast's eagle mid-flight and slammed into the face of her latest poor judgement call claws first. She'd told him off for that. Like all witches, she was well-practiced at the spells to remove memories from non-magical minds, but manufacturing a memory to explain the claw-marks had taken time she could have spent packing up to get the hell out of there.

How many times do I have to tell you that getting burned

when you hook up with deadbeats is not an autoimmune condition? Saifa snapped.

Trinity focussed on sweeping and ignored him. Her grandmother had warned her about the power of three, about how her autoimmune conditions had clumped together. Saifa might be an ancient demon but her Grandmother had foresight. She had seen Trinity's future. Her autoimmune conditions meant she was doomed to be attacked by her body, her power, and her heart. All she needed to do to stay healthy was never eat delicious gluten ever again, spend her life with a shapeshifting demon who could siphon her power away before it destroyed her, and avoid any potential love interests. Oh, and all the witches who would use her as their personal wireless charger if given the chance. So, avoid anyone remotely interesting, basically.

Once again, she had caved and found a warm body to spend the night with at a bar. And once again, it had ended badly. She'd been so careful not to let him have prolonged exposure to her, hoping she could avoid contaminating him with her curse. The latest man had been a damn nurse. He should have been safe. And now she was back to leaving her flat at frantic speed just in case the memory spell didn't take properly and he came back to find her. More of her hard-earned cash sunk into paying out her notice to another landlord. She just needed to accept that she would always be lonely.

Saifa hopped into her lap and bit her hard on the nose.

"Ow! What was that for?"

Your puny human life is short enough without you wasting it sitting around feeling sorry for yourself. You're boring me. Go do something interesting.

"Thanks for the motivational speech. Wanna make a meme to go with that?" Trinity's voice dripped sarcasm as she shoved Saifa away and snatched up the dustpan.

Sure.

Trinity groaned as she watched him transform into a pūriri moth. "I was kidding."

Your life is as short to me as the pūriri moth is to you. It can't eat at all and that doesn't stop it spending its only two days on earth getting laid.

"I get it. Now change back to something I'm not going to accidentally squash."

I'll change back when you get a life. I know your Grandma taught you to keep safe, but not everyone is out to get you. It wouldn't hurt to try hanging out with someone you actually have something in common with. There's a word for people who keep doing the same thing over and over expecting a different result.

Trinity glared at the large green moth on the floor, who twitched his antennae and fluttered over to the door. How could he tell her people weren't out to get her when she was literally cleaning up from someone trying to get her? She swept the glass into a rubbish bag and grabbed her jacket.

"Fine. Let's get out of this town and see if I can find a life in the next one."

That's the spirit.

Saifa waited for her to put her jacket on and then

settled himself on her chest like a brooch. The colours on his wings shifted to look ever-so-slightly less realistic. A hint of metallic sheen veined through the bright greens. He was stunning, but no way in hell would she tell him that. He didn't need any encouragement. Trinity raised her middle finger at him and strode out the door.

As she got into her small four-wheel-drive, she tried not to think about what it said about her that everything she owned could comfortably fit inside it. Two bags of clothes and a bag of magic paraphernalia she hardly used but couldn't bear to part with filled up the seats. Pillows and a duvet were shoved in the boot. Her two most precious possessions were slid down into the footwell and hanging off the tow bar on the back—the computer she made her living from, and the mountain bike she did her living on.

Saifa fluttered off her jacket onto the dash for a better view as Trinity put her seatbelt on. She pulled out of the driveway without another glance at the flat that had been home for the last six months. It was five hours drive to Wellington and she wanted to be there already.

As she skirted the vast crater lake of Taupō she realised how much she had been yearning for the ocean. The endless shifting of the waves matched her life far better than the placid water of this crater. It would be good to be near a coast again. It would be good to explore new trails. It would be good.

What hovel have you found for us this time? Saifa asked.

"It actually looks pretty nice. It's a flat above a bistro. Looks pretty new. It might even be warm and dry."

How far from the nearest mountain bike park? That was almost a rhetorical question. It was the only essential criteria for their constant moves.

"Five minutes' ride max. I was lucky. Someone pulled out of the lease just before I called."

It had been years since Trinity last visited Wellington. She'd still had her Grandma then. She didn't want to think about that. Instead, she let the passing miles and hours lull her into a kind of trance. When they reached the bottom of a speed-trap gorge and turned onto the final stretch of motorway, the view of the harbour took her breath away. White-capped cerulean waters were chased across the harbour by wind gusts that shook the car as they merged with another state highway. Green forested hills held scatterings of houses that clung tight to their curves like baby possums clinging to their mother, despite her frequent efforts to shake them free. Fast approaching was the 'cake tin' stadium that was so flat it looked more like a fat-tyre wheel waiting for an innertube, and beyond that the concrete, glass and height of the CBD. A crushing density of people she had no interest in, although it was nowhere near as bad as Auckland. For a moment her chest tightened and she wondered if she'd made a horrible mistake. She usually avoided cities. There was too much potential for connection there.

She felt better as she turned off the motorway and drove past the low brick wall and towering trees of the botanic gardens. This city was different. There was space to breathe here. It would be OK.

They had driven in silence for the last few hours but as they entered the short Karori tunnel that marked the boundary to the suburb that would be their new home Saifa whirred up from the dashboard, crashing into the windscreen and careening into Trinity's jacket where he clung trembling.

"Saifa! What the hell? Do you want me to crash?" She pulled the car over past the traffic lights on the other side of the tunnel, parking underneath the first of a row of pōhutukawa trees lining the road.

I feel like someone just walked over my grave, he said.

"You're not dead. And even if you were, there wouldn't be a body to bury. There *are* a bunch of other people's bodies buried just around the corner though. Maybe you're feeling the energy from the cemetery," Trinity pointed out, peering at his moth form in concern. It wasn't like him to freak out unless something was very wrong. She peered in her mirrors in case someone had followed them, but the rest of the traffic was carrying on past them without taking any notice. "How do you feel now?"

Saifa flared his wings out and then settled them back down. His antennae were still vibrating. *Fine. I think.*

"Let's find home and then we can figure it out," she said.

He stopped trembling as they took off again, but stayed on her jacket for the rest of the trip. When they crested a rise partway into Karori, they could finally see the valley they would be calling home. She knew the bush in the distance must be Mākara Peak. A communications tower covered in satellite dishes protruded from its summit. The outline of trails curled across the hillside, twisting along the ridgelines. She could feel them calling her, itching to be ridden.

The bistro they would live above was one of those hidden gems off the main road. Hiding was not a great strategy for a business. She missed the turn-off the first time and had to turn back. It was obvious once she found the street, though. A skinny modern building nestled in between the 70's-era houses. The large window frontage was screened by angled, wooden, privacy slats that were new enough to have only weathered halfway to silver. She grinned as she read the sign above the door—Thyme Laud Bistro. Anyone who built a business around a Doctor Who pun was going to be good people in her book.

The small dining space was empty when she walked in. Trinity stopped in the entryway to take it all in.

If you leave your mouth hanging open like that something will fly into it. Saifa said, but she could hear the grudging admiration in his voice.

The space was a chaotic juxtaposition of interior design. It was incredible. A bar leaner ran along the length of the front window, but instead of stools it had swing seats hanging from the ceiling. The walls closest to the entryway held two large panels of colourful stencilled bird artworks that she could see would fold out into tables and chairs if the place got busy. They left the entryway clear and inviting. The stencil artworks were reproduced in some of the oval plywood shapes that cascaded across the ceiling at different heights, along with a scattering of mirrors that reflected the colours and light around the space.

In the back half of the bistro past a few more traditional tables, was a café counter with bar stools overhung by a varying height steel construction that held draping succulents and ferns. On the right, booth seating for four was enclosed in the same kind of wooden slats as the window's privacy screen, but they curved inward together near the ceiling to create a birdcage effect. And on the far back wall were two floor-to-ceiling bookcases. She drifted closer to inspect the titles: a varied collection of science fiction and fantasy magazines along with beautiful hardcovers on food, tiny houses, and interior design.

The clever use of the relatively small space along with the eclectic décor threw her back to memories of the house bus she'd been raised in with her Grandma. She'd only been in the bistro a minute but the feel of the place wrapped around her like a familiar blanket. It was shiny and new but it felt just like the only place she'd ever called home.

"Hello. Can I help you?" a man called from behind the bar.

Trinity started a little, caught snooping at the books, and turned to face him. There was a door behind the bar that he must have come through, presumably leading to the kitchen. He was leaning on the counter, both sleeves rolled up to show forearms muscled from what must be more than just folding the batter for the almond meal chocolate cake sitting on the counter. The rich smell of chocolate was making her mouth water even three steps away. The top two buttons of his shirt were unbuttoned down to the point where they met what she suspected was an all-organic black cotton apron. He looked the type with his perfectly groomed beard and swept-back hair.

"I'm looking for Charlie? I'm renting the flat upstairs," she said.

His polite smile broke into something more genuine that lit up his golden-brown eyes. "That's me. You must be Trinity!" He came out from behind the bar to shake her hand.

Trinity hid her surprise. She'd pictured somebody older to be able to build a place like this. Although now that he was closer, she could see the laugh lines in the corners of his eyes and a handful of silver strands hidden in his hair. His strong hand enveloped hers and her pulse kicked at the touch. She ignored it. Landlords were off limits. Always. She couldn't risk losing all her things to a relationship with a landlord gone wrong. And her relationships always went wrong.

"This place is amazing," she said to distract herself, gesturing around them.

"Thank you. I decided as long as I was overcapitalising I may as well make it something I loved. Something beautiful."

"Well, you succeeded!"

"We'll see. I have to try and make money off it now.

Here are the keys to the bistro and to your place. The lock is just here." He stepped around her and pulled a bookend out of the shelf to reveal a deadbolt. The whole bookshelf swung out as he turned the key.

"That is... I don't even know what that is. The coolest front door I've ever seen," Trinity said.

Charlie smiled again, but this time she could see the hint of envy in his eyes. "Sorry you have to walk through the bistro to get in. If things take off I'll expand the restaurant upstairs one day. In the meantime, I was going to live in the flat myself, but I need the extra rent while I get established. I'm staying at my brother's place in town."

"It takes time to build a customer base. It took me a good few years with my copywriting. You'll get there. Hopefully not before I move on, though!" she joked.

"How long do you think you'll be here?"

"Hard to say. My work is all remote for overseas clients. So, I tend to stay until I get bored of the bike trails and then move on. Do you ride?" she asked.

"Sadly, no. I love running in the park but the bistro takes all my time right now."

Trinity found her eyes had dropped to his lips as he spoke and forced herself to shift her gaze to the counter behind him. "Your food looks as amazing as the bistro. I love that you have gluten-free cake."

The cake is safe for you if you want to spend more time with him. No gluten contamination, Saifa's voice in her mind was suspiciously innocent. Trinity silently cursed his position on her jacket that meant he'd noticed her traitor body's reaction to Charlie's earlier touch.

Don't even go there, she replied.

"Are you coeliac? My sister-in-law is, so I've got a separate fryer and I always make sure to have something around that she can eat," Charlie said.

"Yeah, I am. If that cake's as delicious as it smells I suspect I'll be your number one customer."

Charlie smiled at the compliment and Trinity felt her heart kick again. "As long as you're upstairs I may commandeer you as official taste-tester for my gluten-free experiments. Do you need a hand moving your stuff?"

"I'll be fine, thanks. I don't have much. And I'll happily consume any and all experiments." The words had left her mouth before she had time to kick herself. She should not be offering to spend more time with Charlie. Saifa didn't say anything but she got a distinct sensation of smugness along their connection. She wished he'd picked a larger body so she could kick him.

"Welcome home then, Trinity. I'll let you get settled in."

Saifa flew upstairs once Charlie turned back to the kitchen and Trinity started ferrying her bags from the car.

The flat was much more minimalist than downstairs. The kitchenette was small but the lounge was spacious enough and furnished with a basic grey couch and a coffee table. It was clear Charlie had poured his money into the bistro rather than the upstairs that would be gutted one day to extend his business. The lounge window had a beautiful outlook over the roofs of nearby houses towards the bush reserve, though. As she entered the bedroom, she noticed a skylight above the bed that would let her stare up at the stars at night. She was going to get on just fine living there.

He seemed nice... Saifa said as she threw her duvet and pillows onto the bed.

"Not happening. He's my landlord. Imagine what would happen if he went all possessive on me. No need to smash a window if you have a key," she replied to his suggestive tone and twitching antennae.

You were going to get a life, remember?

"I'll get it somewhere else."

CHAPTER TWO

There were three things Trinity had to do whenever she moved to a new town—set up house, set her wards for protection, and figure out the location of any other witches living in the area. The second and third had been drummed into her repeatedly by her Grandma when they'd travelled from town to town in a cramped house bus in her teens.

"Don't ever let your guard down, Trini," she used to say. "The most dangerous witches are always the ones you don't see coming. Power corrupts and once they realise you have an endless supply, they'll never let you go. Don't let them get close."

Her Grandma was long-gone, but the lesson was habit. The first thing she did that night was set the wards that would keep them safe and map out possible witch locations. She trawled through the local magic community social network using a pseudonym and false address. She noted down each residence on a digital map of the suburb, but she didn't expect anyone truly dangerous to be listed there. To find the real threats she would need to use her power.

She sat up straight on the couch and clicked her back as she stretched before looking around for Saifa. He was sitting near the fairy lights she had strung across her bedhead, letting the body memory of his current form hold him mesmerised by the warm points of light.

"Aren't you bored of being a moth yet?"

Aren't you bored of mothballing your life yet?

Trinity groaned. "Please. Don't start with the moth puns. Come help finish this."

Saifa fluttered over to her neck and she felt the brush of his body against her earlobe as he settled. *Ready?*

Trinity nodded, closing her eyes as she felt him crawl across her face and spread his wings wide to cover her nose and mouth. They knew from experience that there was no way she could risk a spell while she was overflowing with power. Her lips began to tingle as Saifa went to work and then she felt the familiar release of pressure as he siphoned her excess power into himself. He would never admit to it, but she knew he went out of his way to be gentle with her —shifting her power's burning potential between them in a way she always imagined as being like osmosis, a rebalancing between them. When they reached an equilibrium, Saifa shifted down to the arm of the couch where he could see the touchscreen that lay flat on her lap displaying the map of Karori. She could feel him trembling with the effort of controlling himself. There was always a moment after he siphoned where he had to battle his desire to keep feeding and consume her energy completely. It had scared her when she was younger, but he had never given in and she trusted him. She would never risk practising magic without him, not since the fire.

She already had the antique brass dividers she used for mapping magic ready, tipped with conductive foam to form a stylus. Next to Saifa was the rest of the DIY spell kit she had cobbled together from what was available. She couldn't wander into a magical supply shop like a normal witch, although she wished she could because she'd heard Witch Way Magical Supplies in Thorndon was amazing. Instead, an old disc brake formed the weight of the pendulum she hung from her hands with brake cables. She pushed the dividers through its centre and waited for Saifa to fly down and perch on the metal circle before holding it over the map. They had worked this spell together a dozen times or more, an adaptation of a standard locating spell that incorporated her demon familiar's natural talent for finding sources of the power that he fed upon. It wouldn't find someone determined to hide, but it did just fine at finding anyone they needed to steer clear of in the neighbourhood.

Trinity and Saifa's whispered chanting twined together, hers breaking the silence of the apartment and his breaking the silence of her mind. The divider swayed over the screen, pausing as it pulled at an unnatural angle away from her. She carefully lowered the pendulum until the stylus marked an address on Birdwood Street at the outskirts of the map. There should have been more to mark, but the disc had started jerking wildly over the screen. They kept the spell going a minute longer but every time the pendulum moved towards the centre of the map, it spun out of control.

"Weird. It's never done that before. It's like there's a whirlpool in the middle and the spell can only function on the edges," Trinity said, frowning.

Can moths puke? I think I'm going to be sick, Saifa whimpered in her mind.

Trinity grabbed the disk brake to stop its spinning and let the now visibly shaking moth topple into her hand. "Sorry. I didn't think."

I noticed.

Trinity knew that tone of voice. It was best to give him some space when he got in that mood. She left the computer running a search for images of the residents of the addresses they'd found. Saifa would memorise the faces while she slept and warn her if they started coming across any of them too often when they were out.

Trinity stumbled as she stood up to go to bed and threw out a hand to brace herself on the wall as the room spun. She hardly worked any magic for fear of discovery and she was out of practice. Even that simple spell had left her exhausted. Or maybe it was that roiling energy that had spun the pendulum that she was feeling. She staggered the few steps to the bedroom and slipped under the duvet without bothering to take her clothes off. She could smell a hint of mildew from the covers, a reminder of the damp flat they'd left that morning. The last thing she saw before succumbing to a dreamless sleep was Mars glowing bright beneath the waning crescent moon.

The next morning, as she perched on a barstool of the bistro downstairs and washed down her freshly baked gluten-free cheese scone with the perfect flat white coffee for breakfast, she managed to let go of a little of the tension she had been carrying as an ache across her shoulders. When the warning signs had started at the bar the other night she'd ignored them, too tired from years of itinerant living to face another move. She should have recognised the tell-tale shift in behaviour. The hard grip of his hand on her shoulder when he put his arm around her. The jealous glares he'd thrown out to anyone who came near. It wasn't the first time she'd seen that kind of thing. When he'd come back the next night to her Taupō flat, she'd refused to open the door to him and he'd crashed in through the window. She'd honestly felt more irritated than scared.

"What are you frowning about?" Charlie asked as he returned from the kitchen. He was carrying an orange cake covered in candied rind and slivered almonds that shone under the lights from the sticky sugary glaze it had been drizzled with.

"Nothing. I'm just thinking how lucky I am to end up

living right above somewhere I can actually eat," Trinity said, pushing the dark thoughts aside to smile at him.

Charlie raised a doubtful eyebrow and then let it go. He obviously wasn't fooled by her deflection. Trinity reminded herself not to let her guard down just because the man could bake safe food. She'd had Saifa check everything on the bench when he was out in the kitchen and had been surprised that there wasn't a single glutenous crumb.

"What's the verdict on the scone? I usually stick to cakes for the counter food but I thought you'd probably need some breakfast."

"I'd say it sits somewhere between delicious and exquisite. Thank you. I haven't had a proper scone since I was living with my Grandma," Trinity said, suppressing the tears that tried to push themselves up at the thought. Something about this place was bringing back all sorts of memories. *Landlord. He's your landlord. Don't make it weird,* she reminded herself.

Charlie grabbed a scone for himself and came to sit with her. "How long ago was that?"

The sight of his strong hands tearing the scone apart distracted her for a moment. Then she pushed away the ridiculous analogy of Captain America tearing apart a log of wood and forced herself to focus.

Maybe it was the kindness and genuine interest in his face. Maybe it was the weird way this space felt like home. Maybe she was just tired and lonely. Whatever the reason, she found herself inexplicably speaking actual truths about her past. Something she normally avoided at all costs. "I lived with her for most of my childhood until she died when I was 20. She had this crazy house bus and life was all kinds of weird, but every Sunday morning I'd wake up to the smell of scones baking and we'd have Devonshire Tea in bed for breakfast."

"Proper Devonshire Tea? With clotted cream?" Charlie asked, sounding intrigued.

"Yup. We were on the road so we were never far from a dairy farm and she'd had years to get a network of suppliers set up for her weekly fix."

Charlie laughed. "You make her sound like a drug dealer. I think I would have liked her. I love buying from the farmgate and that kind of simple really good food is what makes life worth living."

"I agree. Sadly, the baking genes skipped my generation, which is why I have been sconeless since she passed." Sconeless and lonely. She loved Saifa. He was the only family she had left. But the demon wasn't human. She couldn't sit and share a meal with him and he couldn't wrap his arms around her and hold her when she was sad because he didn't have any. The damn tears wouldn't stay put this time and she had to sneakily wipe the dampness from her cheek. She straightened up and forced her thoughts away from the painful memories.

Charlie must have noticed because he launched into a hilarious story from his own childhood and soon she was too busy laughing to be sad. He was so easy to talk to. They talked right through another cup of coffee each.

"What are your plans for the day?" he asked as she drained the last sip from her cup.

"I'm going to go for a ride to pick up some groceries and then I need to get some work done for a client," she said.

"There's not much in the fridge up there. Will you be able to carry everything on your bike? I could give you a ride."

Did you hear that Trini? He could give you a ride, Saifa murmured into her mind suggestively, as if he could tell exactly what she'd been picturing a moment earlier.

Shut up, Trinity thought back at him even though she knew he was just trying to help distract her. She took a bite of scone drenched in butter to cover her blush. "I don't need a ride, thanks. I've got my car if I need it but I prefer biking. I fully intend to take advantage of having you here... I mean your bistro... having your bistro here," she said.

Charlie smiled again and she couldn't look away from his golden-brown eyes. "Well, I could definitely use the extra custom. Business has been slower than I hoped. Is there anything you're craving?"

Trinity choked on the piece of scone she was still swallowing and grabbed her coffee to try and wash it down. The blush was infinitely worse now but at least she had the choking as an excuse. Charlie reached out and placed a hand on her back, looking concerned. "Are you alright?"

Trinity nodded, breathing in very slowly before coughing as hard as she could to dislodge the crumb that had tried to block her windpipe.

"So, any requests then?" Charlie asked. His hand was still resting lightly on her back.

"I don't suppose you've ever tried your hand at cronuts? I miss them so much," Trinity said, talking too fast. Why had she said that? She didn't expect him to become her personal bakery.

Charlie looked thoughtful. "Now that would be a challenge. Gluten-free pastry can be tricky. But I make a killer lemon curd I could inject into them."

Hear that? He wants to inject your donuts.

Trinity forced her face to stay neutral and wished she could mentally kick Saifa. *Shut up,* she told him again. She stood up and brushed her hands down her shirt nervously. "That sounds amazing. I'd better get going. Lots to do," she said.

Charlie smiled again and she couldn't help but return it. "Have fun. The Karori supermarkets are quite small. If you can't find what you need, head down to Thorndon New World," he said.

"Thanks. See you later."

"For dinner?" he asked.

Trinity paused, half-turned away from him. *Landlord. He's your landlord.* "Not tonight, sorry. I'll probably work late," she said. Her resolve crumbled as she saw the disappointment in his face, though. "Definitely soon, though. I haven't forgotten my taste-testing obligations!"

Charlie waved goodbye as she left.

So, when's soon? Tomorrow? Saifa said as she grabbed her bike from the garage.

Shut up.

You really need to work on your mental vocabulary.

Trinity rolled her eyes.

IT FELT good to be back on two wheels. She hadn't ventured out of her old flat for the last week she'd been in it and she had started going stir-crazy. Even the ubiquitous Wellington wind pushing against her didn't put her off. It swept the hair from her eyes and blew new breath into her lungs. She couldn't bring herself to stop when she reached the Karori supermarkets and headed for Thorndon New World like Charlie suggested, instead.

She dutifully kept an eye out for the witch's house that the pendulum had pointed to the night before but all she could see when they passed it was a moss-covered letterbox. The house was hidden from view down below the street.

Her mind finally cleared as she sped down the hill towards the tunnel out of Karori. She ignored how fast she must be going as the world became a blur, revelling in the motion. Her fingers clenched on the brakes in frustration when she reached the red light at the bottom. There were no traffic lights in the bush. She couldn't wait to get back on the trails. As she waited for the light to change, she looked over at the pōhutukawa trees they'd seen the day before. It already felt familiar. This move was going to be different from all the others. She could feel it. Or she could feel her own desperate hope at least.

Saifa had tucked himself under her jacket for the ride with just his antennae poking up near her zip. As they neared the Karori tunnel she felt something from him. Not a physical tremble, there was too much other movement to feel that, more a vibration in her mind. As they entered the shadow of the archway she heard his scream in her head and slammed on the brakes. Instinct made her throw her weight backward and avoid a headfirst trip over the handlebars. A flurry of green wings slapped her face as Saifa shot from her jacket back the way they'd come. The honking of the car behind her ricocheted off the tunnel walls and just about deafened her.

She blinked and then turned back to scan the air for Saifa. A car bumper was inches from her rear tyre and the driver was yelling out the window. The bus coming the other way had stopped as well, probably wondering if the crazy cyclist was going to veer into oncoming traffic. She got off her bike and turned it back towards Karori, still dazed. She was barely inside the tunnel's bounds and it only took a few seconds to walk back out into the sunshine. She kept walking until she reached the footpath beyond, ignoring the angry looks of the passing drivers who she'd held up. Saifa found her sunk down into a crouch on the pavement leaning back against a low wooden fence several long minutes later.

"What the hell was that? Where the hell have you been?"

Didn't you feel it? There's a barrier at the tunnel that I can't pass. It stretches either side as well. I'm trapped here. Someone's trapped us here. His words were too fast and his voice in her mind was thick with rage.

"You don't know that for sure. Slow down and explain."

I can't travel down any of the streets that leave Karori from here. I doubt the bush tracks will be any better. I can feel the barrier curving outwards into the distance. This suburb is a cage.

"Can you fly over it?"

I can't fly higher than Mākara Peak without hitting a wall of power.

"What? Who would do that?"

I don't know. But that must be why the pendulum went crazy. It sensed the trap.

Trinity shivered in the warmth of the late morning sunshine. She'd always kept ahead of anyone who might use her by running, but she might have just run herself right into someone's grasp. Saifa was shaking uncontrollably.

"Are you okay? What did it do to you?"

I'm fine. I just kept testing the boundaries and it weakened me.

"Take some of my power and go home and rest. I can get the groceries without you."

It was an indication of how weakened he was that he didn't protest. He would never usually let her out of sight in a new location. She buried her head between her knees to let him crawl across her mouth without anyone seeing. The magic burned as it passed between them with the pressure of a flash flood. He had lost the ability to moderate the process in his stress. She was still reeling when he took off to fly home. She caught a glimpse of feathers from the corner of her vision as he changed to an avian shape to speed the journey. She wished she had the heart to rub his nose in the fact he hadn't stayed a moth. Instead, she stood and swung her leg over the bike to start the climb back up to Karori proper and the local supermarkets. She didn't want to leave the suburb without him.

CHAPTER THREE

Trinity couldn't focus as she weaved her way up and down the supermarket aisles grabbing the bare minimum to get her through the next few days. She gave up partway down the third aisle when she couldn't find what she needed and swapped to the other supermarket. What genius had taken a perfectly sized supermarket space and divided it into two inadequate stores? She needed to figure out what was trapping Saifa fast or she could foresee a lot of solo outings to a decent grocery store in her future.

Thinking of poor Saifa filled her with nervous energy and she spun her shopping trolley around towards the checkout to leave. She could do a better shop some other time. She needed to get home. She was in such a hurry that she didn't notice the man who'd been behind her until it was too late. The end of her trolley hit him in the arm.

"Ow!" said a rich tenor voice.

"I'm so sorry! Are you OK?" Trinity abandoned the trolley to approach him and then stood awkwardly wondering what the protocol was when you accidentally rammed into a gorgeous man in the supermarket. She caught a glimpse of a Rolex on his writs and winced a little. Make that gorgeous and rich. Ugh. Gorgeous rich men were the worst. She'd only made that mistake once. It was much harder hiding from someone with enough money to track you.

The man peered down at his arm and undid the cufflink on his crisp white collared shirt to roll his sleeve up and check the damage. "Can't see any damage. I've had worse bailing off my bike," he said, smiling as he turned his tanned forearm towards her to display a half-healed graze.

"You ride?" Trinity said, unable to quite keep the disbelief from her voice as she tried to picture the too-perfectly groomed man in his tailored designer shirt and suit pants on a mountain bike with mud splattered up his back. He looked more like a gym-bunny. She was sure he'd picked the close-fitting shirt to show off his biceps. The lines of black waxed cord from some kind of pendant that hung out of sight were the only suggestion that this clean-shaven businessman might not be as straight-laced as he appeared.

"Every moment I can. You?" he asked.

"Every moment plus some I can't," Trinity said, finally cracking a smile.

The man went to roll his sleeve back down and dropped his cufflink in the process. Trinity crouched down to pick it up for him and their hands brushed as they both grabbed for it at the same time. A tingle spread up her arm from the contact.

"Sorry. You must be magnetic or something. I keep running into you." She smiled again and told herself off for not shifting back to make the distance between them more comfortable. He had the most intriguing grey-blue eyes, old beyond his years and focussed completely on her.

"Well, I'm afraid you'll have to make it up to me by taking me for a ride up Salvation this afternoon."

Was she imagining the suggestion in that sentence? It must be the day for it. She could only assume she was giving off desperate lonely vibes. How embarrassing. She usually had no problem avoiding connecting with the people she met and here she was interacting with two men in one day. Maybe her brain had finally broken. She breathed deep to keep the blush at bay and stood back up. "I don't know the trails around here yet," she prevaricated. It was only half true. She'd ridden many of the tracks on past visits. She was pretty sure Salvation headed up Wrights Hill.

"Perfect. It's a date then," he said, popping his cufflink back in without taking his eyes off hers. "I'll meet you at the bottom entrance at two."

She opened her mouth to say she didn't even know his name, but he was already sauntering away. There was no other word for the way he moved. She pursed her lips and glared at his entitled, over-dressed, perfectly formed behind. That kind of confidence drove her nuts. She hated it... loved to hate it. There was something different about him, though. She'd caught a hint of the same loneliness she felt when she'd looked into his eyes, a reflection of pain like hers hiding underneath his cockiness. She checked her watch. She had just under an hour to get home, eat some lunch and get to the trail. Damn him. At least if she was with him she wouldn't be getting herself into trouble with her landlord.

Charlie was busy serving customers when she got back to the flat with her groceries. She tipped her head in greeting as she wandered through the bistro with her panniers. A search of her small living space when she'd finished putting everything away turned up no sign of Saifa anywhere. She frowned in concern. She wasn't too worried yet, but if he wasn't back by this evening she'd have too much power built up to safely search for him. She bit her lip as she tried to decide what to do and then glanced at the clock—1:30 p.m. Maybe a bike ride was just what she needed to take her mind off things. Saifa would show up when he was ready. He was quite capable of taking care of himself.

Trinity arrived at the entrance of the Salvation trail bang on 2 p.m. She'd looked up the map before she left and saw it connected in a loop to a downhill trail called Deliverance that exited not far from where she was standing. She stared up at the bush and watched two kākā soaring near a distant high voltage power pylon. Their squawking cries echoed down the valley.

The man from the supermarket was five minutes late. If she hadn't heard the soft crunch of gravel under the tyres of his electric car, she wouldn't have noticed him pull in behind where she was waiting. She barely kept her sarcastic groan to herself when she saw his car. It was a showy metallic-green electric Porsche with a matching custom-everything carbon-frame mountain bike on the roof rack. No wonder he'd seemed so entitled. At least he wouldn't try and borrow money from her. Not that she'd be seeing him again anyway she promised herself.

"Sorry I'm late. Some lady crashed into my arm at the supermarket," he said, as he got out of the car.

Trinity rolled her eyes. "Can you actually ride that thing or is it just to co-ordinate with the car?"

"Ouch! Adding insult to my trolley injury?"

Trinity shrugged and ignored the question. She probably could have been nicer but the man exuded arrogance and she kind of liked the mischief that flashed in his eyes when he responded to her verbal assault. She would have been distracted by the sight of his arms flexing as he lifted his bike down if she hadn't already been drooling over the bike. She could never afford anything like it. At least if he couldn't ride it properly, she should be able to leave him in the dust down Deliverance and not look back. "I'm Trinity, by the way. In case you were wondering."

The man grinned. "Names are such a commitment. I didn't want to get too attached before I made sure you could actually ride. I'm Dante. Ready?" he asked, as he strapped a full-face enduro helmet on.

Trinity rolled her eyes and took off up the track without bothering to reply, setting a solid pace. There was no way she'd turn down that sort of a challenge. She'd checked the gradient and altitude of the track on the map before she left and knew from experience exactly how hard she could push herself. If he couldn't keep up that was his problem. The filtered green light of the bush, soft breeze, and rustling birdsong of the tūī and pīwakawaka made her forget her irritation within minutes. She never felt better than when she was deep in the bush riding a trail. She settled down into her seat and focussed on the rhythm of her pedalling, her own unique form of meditation. The stress of the incident at the tunnel finally dissipated, for a while at least. Her controlled breathing as she responded to the undulations and switchbacks of the track chased away the tightness in her chest.

She looked back over her shoulder as she reached a break in the canopy that let the sunshine through. The sudden warmth on her face set her sweating. Dante and his metallic green bike were two lengths behind her, keeping up with ease. She grinned to herself and shifted gears to push faster. As they reached the first branch in the trail, a baby quail ran across the path and dove for cover down the bushy hillside. She could smell the damp leaves they were disturbing and a hint of wood smoke from a house below them. This was living.

When they reached the car park at the top, Trinity was breathing hard and she could feel that wonderful ache in her legs from a great climb. She shook her hands out as she sat upright on her bike staring out across the hills to the sparkling harbour beyond.

Dante stopped beside her, his knee just brushing hers, and pulled his helmet off. "Not bad, huh?"

"I didn't realise you could see the ocean from up here. It's so nice to see it again."

"Did you move recently?" he asked.

"Yeah. Yesterday."

"Where'd you come from?"

"Up north," Trinity answered vaguely. She didn't like talking about where she'd been, just like she didn't like talking about where she was going. She couldn't afford to leave any loose ends that might catch up with her.

Dante leaned closer to her and pointed to an island in the distance. "That's Matiu/Somes Island. It's a nice day trip on the ferry on a good day. We should go sometime."

Trinity turned to face him. "Most guys ask for a number first, you know," she said.

He grinned and leaned back to take a long drink from his water bottle. "Can I have your number?"

"Maybe. Let's see how you go downhill," Trinity said, taking off before he could notice how annoyingly charming she found him.

She was almost back across the car park before Dante caught her up, launching his bike airborne to balance on his back wheel on one of the low fence posts before bunny-hopping onto the start of the single-track ahead of her.

"Show off," she muttered to herself. But as they charged down the steep drops and stream crossings of the downhill trail, she couldn't help but grin.

It wasn't a super technical track, but Dante was more

familiar with it. He was out of sight within minutes and was sitting in the grass with his bike already on the roof rack by the time she reached the bottom. She dismounted next to him and took her helmet off to lay back on the grass soaking up the sunshine with her eyes closed. She could feel the warm power of the earth beneath her and for the first time in weeks, she felt grounded. She breathed in deeply and let it out again.

"Feeling better?" he asked.

"Why do you think I was feeling bad?" she replied, shading her eyes to look up at him.

"You looked anxious and distracted in the store. Or do you usually crash into people like that?"

She scrunched her face up. "You're not going to let me forget that are you? Yes. I feel better. Thanks."

"Does that mean I can have your number then?" he asked. He stretched his legs out and rolled onto his side to watch her.

Trinity found herself staring into his grey-blue eyes again, intrigued by the hidden complexity she could sense in them. She could see a slight tension in his jaw as he waited for her answer. At least he wasn't assuming anything. Maybe he wasn't as arrogant as he seemed.

"Yeah, I guess so," she said, careful to keep her voice casual and wondering what on earth she was doing. But maybe Saifa was right. Maybe the problem was that she kept finding deadbeats. Dante might be a little cocky but he was clearly no deadbeat. There was no harm in going for a few rides. She could always ignore him when he tried to contact her. Plus, he had the added bonus of not being her landlord. She winced a little at that thought. She was pretty sure not being her landlord shouldn't really be the main criteria for whether to hang out with a guy.

"Want a lift home?" he asked. His eyes had shifted down to her lips.

Trinity stood up and grabbed her helmet before she did something she regretted. "Nah. I'm good."

Dante held her bike upright for her while she put her helmet on. "It was lovely to meet you, Trinity."

Those grey-blue eyes had captured hers again, inviting her closer. Her mind started drifting and she distracted herself with mounting her bike. Why couldn't she seem to stay focussed? "Yeah, nice to meet you. See you 'round."

"Try not to crash into my car on the way past. It's magnetic too."

She glared at him for bringing up her embarrassing words from the trolley accident and he laughed. He hadn't moved away when she'd taken her bike back off him and she had to crane her neck up to look at him. She could smell the forest on him. What kind of man smelled that good after a hard ride? The pendant she'd noticed earlier had fallen out of his shirt. It was a hexagonal disk of shining black obsidian. She reached up to touch it without thinking, feeling its power calling to her, drawing her in. For a moment she wondered if he was a witch but she dismissed the thought as soon as it entered her mind. No witch would draw attention to himself the way his displays of wealth did and she hadn't noticed any hint of power when she touched his skin. It must just be the natural power of the volcanic glass she was feeling. She'd always been sensitive to that kind of thing.

"You're not one of those new-age crystal types are you?" she teased. She'd always wondered how anyone, witches especially, could handle having crystals next to their skin, but her grandma had told her not everyone felt them quite like she did. And non-magical people didn't feel them at all, of course.

Dante laughed. "No. It reminds me of a place that's special to me," he said in explanation, brushing her hand with his as he reached up to tuck the pendant back beneath his shirt.

WHEN SHE GOT BACK to her flat, Saifa still hadn't returned. She stripped off her gear and jumped in the shower. If he wasn't back by the time she got out, she would scry for him. The ride had drained her anxiety away and left her calm and focussed.

Her moth companion fluttered in the open window of the lounge while she was towelling her hair dry.

"Where have you been?" Trinity demanded as soon as she saw him.

Testing the boundaries of the barrier. It encircles the whole suburb, from Mākara peak along the ridgelines of the surrounding hills and right to the far edge of the cemetery. I can't fly higher than the peak anywhere above the suburb. There must be something anchoring it.

"Who would have that kind of power?"

I don't know, but I can't be the only creature trapped by it. The more pressing question is who does it want? Are we the target or just the bycatch?

"Do you think it's the witch we scried on Birdwood Street?"

Maybe. The house stinks of recent spell-work. Saifa sounded doubtful though.

"Well. We can look into him tomorrow. I need to get an article submitted by midnight. Come siphon from me. You look exhausted."

Trinity sat down on the couch and pulled her computer onto her lap as Saifa fluttered over to her face. When she was younger, he'd only had to siphon her power once or twice a week. Her power had grown as she aged and thankfully so had his appetite. Even in the comparatively tiny moth body that he currently inhabited, she could feel the size of his presence from the other planes he existed within. Mostly she found that reassuring. He protected her and in her solitary existence the sensation of his presence filling the lonely spaces of her life was a comfort. But sometimes she wondered what would happen when she died. Wondered where that now vast appetite would be directed. That was future Trinity's problem though. Right then, Saifa needed sustenance and she needed to release the pent-up energy that her traitorous body over-produced.

The familiar tingle of her lips from the transference started as soon as she felt his soft body against her skin and stretched throughout her nervous system tickling her synapses. He had over-exerted himself testing the cage that held him and he was depleted. He was drawing in the equivalent of magical gulps. She forced down a moment of fear at the surge of power between them from his ravenous connection.

"Ow!" she yelled, voice muffled by his deep green and gold form spread across her face. The ache of draining energy had turned to a fiery flash of pain radiating from her heart that she felt in every cell of her body. She tried to draw in a sharp breath and her nostrils were blocked by the flexible membranes of his wings. The burning sensation grew unbearable and her hands tore at her face as she started panicking.

She saw him transform into something large and shadowy for a moment. He was too close for her eyes to focus and see what he'd become. And then he was a pūriri again, perched trembling on the arm of the couch.

Trinity drew in deep gulping breaths and fought the crushing fatigue and dizziness that threatened to sweep her away. "What..." she said weakly

I'm sorry. I was so hungry and I didn't realise your power was drained already. Did you cast something this afternoon while I was out?

"No! I wouldn't risk that. How much?" She was too tired for full sentences.

You had maybe half the power you normally would, Saifa

said. His voice still shook with hunger, but beneath that Trinity could hear concern for her.

"Am I sick or something?"

The timing will not be a coincidence. I don't think we're a bycatch. I think someone's trapped you here to use your power.

"I could leave and try and free you from outside."

You wouldn't last long without me. And I won't last long without something else to eat if this continues. You'd have to return and whoever it is would be waiting. Saifa had fluttered to the window as he said that last sentence.

"Where are you going?"

To hunt. I need food.

"Saifa!"

Not a witch or anything sentient. I'll find one of the other creatures trapped by the spell.

"But..."

Don't worry. I'll make sure it's something dangerous, something expendable. I swore an oath to you. I'm not going to break it.

Trinity's face was drawn with worry as she watched him flit out of the window and disappear into shadow. He hadn't fed on anyone or anything else since they'd sworn to each other. They needed to break the barrier fast. She didn't know how many bad creatures were trapped in the night here, but there couldn't be many or someone would have noticed by now. It wouldn't take long for Saifa to run out of morally unambiguous prey, especially now that his appetite was so much bigger than it used to be.

CHAPTER FOUR

Trinity woke with a groan the next morning. It had taken her until 2 a.m. to drag the words out of herself for her deadline. Better late than never. Saifa had returned sometime after midnight glowing faintly blue. She hadn't asked him why.

Morning, Sunshine. What are we doing about this barrier today?

Saifa's voice thrummed with power making her head vibrate. She groaned again. "I need coffee."

Trinity prised her eyes open and stared up at the grey pensive clouds threatening rain. It was like the skylight was a mirror for her brain.

Coffee, and then surveillance on Mr Birdwood Street so we can cross him off the suspect list.

"Fine."

Trinity stumbled to the bathroom and turned the water pressure of the shower head up as high as it went. The needles of water against her body drove away the last of the fogginess from her mind and by the time she stepped out she felt almost awake. Saifa was waiting on her closet door. She pulled on jeans and a t-shirt before reaching into the back of the closet for the small box she'd tucked away there. This wasn't the first time they'd had to keep a quiet eye on a witch living nearby. If she ever got bored of copywriting maybe she'd go into business as an arcane spy.

A couple of micro-cameras and a charm to pass unnoticed should do it. It's a small house.

"Why don't you fly ahead and let me know when he leaves for work?"

You want some alone time with Charlie? Saifa teased.

Trinity rolled her eyes and tucked the things she needed into the inside pocket of her jacket. "It's a busy road and there's nowhere much to hide. It's safer for you to do it alone. Just call me when he's gone, okay?"

Enjoy, Saifa said as he fluttered out the window.

The bistro was empty when Trinity emerged through the bookcase door a few minutes later, but the mouthwatering smell of fresh lemon and butter filled the space. She stood for a moment with her eyes closed just breathing.

The door to the kitchen was open and Trinity stepped behind the counter to stand on the threshold. Charlie had his back towards her leaning over the gleaming stainless steel bench. His movements were smooth and certain like he had an internal rhythm he was keeping time to. Trinity lost herself watching him, the shift of his muscles as he reached for a piping bag, the tilt of his head as he concentrated on his creations.

She cleared her throat, conscious she had been staring unnoticed for too long. He spun in surprise, perfectly balanced. She'd briefly thought he moved like a dancer with that rhythm, but the way he reacted to the surprise of her presence made her reassess. His feet shifted as he pivoted and one arm drifted up between them before he grinned in recognition. He was a fighter, or a martial artist at least. Her Grandma had signed her up to self-defence classes in every town they'd stopped in for more than a week so she could recognise the way he balanced his weight poised to lunge forward. She really should have kept up with those classes.

"Sorry. I didn't mean to startle you," she said.

"Perfect timing! These are still warm," he replied. The moment of tension left his body like it had never happened and he grabbed two plates from the nearby shelves and placed a pastry on each.

Trinity's eyes widened. "You actually made cronuts? You're amazing! You didn't have to do that."

She moved away from the door to let him through and he placed the plates down in the booth seat nestled in the back corner of the bistro.

"Need a coffee?" he asked.

"Desperately."

He set the coffee grinder going and the intoxicating smell of coffee beans drifted to join the scents of lemon and sugar-crusted pastry. She'd closed her eyes again without realising, immersing herself in the sensations. When she opened them, Charlie was watching her with a smile as he twisted the portafilter into position.

"You look like you're basking in something," he said.

"I am. Culinary artistry and anticipation."

Charlie laughed. "It's nice to be appreciated."

She grabbed the coffees when he was finished and slid into the booth seat, resisting the urge to keep sliding around until she was pressed up against him. She felt a moment of anxiety as she looked down at her plate and belatedly realised there was no Saifa there to tell her if it was safe. But it was too late to back out now. Everything had been fine yesterday and at least she would have time to leave before she got sick if something was contaminated with gluten. Any other thoughts were banished as she bit through sweet, crisp pastry into the soft, citrusy lemon centre. Her eyes were half-closed in pleasure as she washed the first bite down with hot, rich perfectly extracted coffee.

"Do you need a moment alone with that?" Charlie teased, taking a bite of his own.

Trinity blushed and was immediately annoyed at herself. What was she, sixteen? She needed to get a grip. And they needed to be strictly professional. "Nah. It's better with someone watching," her traitor of a mouth said.

Even as she mentally kicked herself for saying something that could have come right out of Saifa's mouth, she couldn't help watching in amusement as he choked on his coffee. Was the faint redness in his cheeks all from the coughing fit or was he blushing too? Cute. No, not cute. Landlords aren't cute, she reminded herself.

"Well, if you can find a way to get some more people in here to watch I could use the extra customers. My sister-in-law told me she's pregnant last night so my free accommodation now has a deadline. Plus, I need to start making some profit so I can spoil my little niece or nephew rotten."

Trinity was almost as surprised at the stab of panic she felt at the thought she might have to move again so soon as she was at the stab of jealousy she felt for the closeness he had with his family. She didn't get attached to places and she certainly didn't get attached to people. So, what was that ache in her chest about? "Congratulations!" she said, pushing the unfamiliar feelings away. "I'm sure we can get the bistro raking it in before you need to move out of your brother's place. Money can't buy the kind of ambience you have here, your food is exceptional, and you're a marketer's wet dream with the way you talk about what you do. You've got the whole package. You just need everyone to see it."

"We? You want to help?" Charlie asked, and she felt the warmth in his eyes wrap around her.

Shit. She never promised something she didn't intend to deliver. Not only was she not supposed to be getting any more involved in Charlie's life, helping him would probably mean she had to move out even sooner. She opened her mouth to say something non-committal and time-limited, but she couldn't do it. "Of course! I can't have my cronut-fix supplier going out of business when I've only just found you!"

"Trinity, I can't accept your help. I can't afford to pay you and you can't make a living if you're giving your services away for free."

"Nonsense. Most of what you need isn't copywriting and seeing the inner workings of a restaurateur will be great research for my next novel. You can pay me in baked goods for any writing I do and anything else is just me helping out a friend."

Charlie stared at her for a long moment and she could see him struggling with his conscience. "No. That's not fair. I'll drop the rent by $50 a week. Keep a tally of what I owe you, and I'll pay you back any shortfall when your confidence in my business pays off."

Trinity frowned. "Can you afford to do that?"

Charlie looked insulted. "How bad a businessman do you think I am? Yes, I can afford it. I wouldn't have offered otherwise."

Trinity sighed. Great. Was she really going to make him a client as well as a landlord? "Alright. But I'm not charging you for anything except copywriting and you're not paying me back until you are making enough profit to afford proper accommodation. I meant what I said."

Charlie smiled. "I'm glad you meant it. I like you. I want us to be friends."

Trinity couldn't help but smile back. Oh crap. This was not going at all how it should be. They couldn't be friends. If they were friends and her power corrupted him it would hurt too much. She'd just have to make sure there was no chance of contaminating him. No touching. She swallowed hard and took another bite of her pastry to distract herself just as she felt a cool tendril of connection wend into her mind from Saifa.

Mr Birdwood Street has just pulled out of the drive. No rush if you're getting busy with Charlie. Even from the other side of the suburb, she could hear the suggestion in his voice.

I will NOT be getting busy with Charlie, she mind-growled back at him, but he had already cut the connection between them. She'd never mastered the ability to find his mind to speak to when he was more than a few metres away from her, which meant she couldn't reply unless he let her. Bastard.

"Where did you go just then? You were staring into the distance and frowning," Charlie said, his head tilting to the side just like when he'd been concentrating on his creations before.

"Sorry, I just realised I'm late for a thing," she said before she got herself into any more trouble. She sculled the rest of her coffee and grabbed the cronut to eat on the way out to her bike. "How much do I owe you?" she said

"Don't be silly. You're taste-testing for me, remember? What's the verdict?"

"Perfect in every way and highly addictive," she said, much like its baker was proving to be. She shook the thought away. She needed to get a grip and focus on the real danger, the trap she'd blindly stepped into.

Charlie grinned at the compliment and took their

coffee cups back to the counter. Trinity stood and surreptitiously checked the spy cameras were still safely tucked away in her pocket while his back was turned. When she turned back to say goodbye, he was close enough that she felt like she was sinking into eyes that were the same rich dark brown as her coffee had been. She let herself drown in them for a split second before glancing away.

"Thank you. I don't get to eat anything like that very often. Have a great day." She winced internally at how banal she sounded.

"You're welcome. I don't get to bake for anyone so gratifying very often," Charlie said.

"When you get a chance, email me through your business plan and any thoughts you have on marketing stuff and I can get started on some web copy and ideas."

"Thank you," Charlie said as he side-stepped around her to finish clearing the table. His hand brushed hers as he passed. She ignored the warmth that contact sent through her and strode towards the door. So much for not touching him. She'd be more careful next time. Except there shouldn't be a next time. She was so screwed. She avoided making eye contact as she waved goodbye.

SAIFA WAS HIDDEN on the back of the white fence railing when Trinity pulled up outside the house of the witch they were checking out. She had slipped the charm against being noticed around her neck when she was still a couple of minutes away. It didn't make her invisible as such, it just meant she wouldn't trigger any warning spells and even if he realised he'd been visited, the witch shouldn't be able to trace her. Grey moonstone for clouding and protection, a derailleur to shift unwanted attention, and a native skink tail for camouflage (secured without killing the lizard of course), all suspended from muka fibre from the harakeke flax for cloaking and to stop any record of her presence bleeding into her surroundings.

The house was lower than the road, nestled in the bush at the bottom of a flight of steep uneven concrete stairs. Saifa fluttered onto her jacket as she started her descent. She waited until she was out of sight of the road before tucking her bike in the bush, just in case they needed to hide in a hurry. The sun hadn't reached the house yet and the air smelled damp from wet moss and leaf litter. Trinity stayed in the bush as she crept closer until she could see the front door and surrounding walls. A small high frosted glass window was ajar to the left of the entrance, probably a bathroom or laundry.

I'll fly them in. No point risking you tripping an alarm spell or something, Saifa said.

Trinity nodded and fished the wireless micro-cameras out of her jacket pocket. "One in the lounge, one in the bedroom?" She asked.

That should do it. Saifa shifted into a bird, one of the ubiquitous kākā, and grasped a camera in each claw before flying down to the window. He struggled for a moment, trying to manoeuvre himself through the gap before dropping to the ground and changing into a greater short-tailed bat to make it easier. The smaller body meant he had to make two trips to get the cameras inside, but his hands were much more dextrous in the mammalian form.

Trinity rolled her eyes at his insistence on only taking the form of native New Zealand species. There were any number of mammals he could have taken the shape of that would have been easier for the job and she was pretty sure he wasn't an endemic demon if there even was such a thing. It wasn't like an extinct nocturnal bat would go unnoticed if he were caught. She sat anxiously counting the minutes as she waited for him to return. The sun was making the dew on the roofing iron steam by the time he emerged.

"What took you so long?" she hissed. She lifted her bike carefully to avoid leaving a record of their presence in broken branches and hauled it back up the steps.

I took a look around once they were set up. He's definitely practising. He has a room of advanced spell-casting equipment. I couldn't find any sign of an anchor for the barrier, but I did find this.

Trinity glanced over at his fluttering form, an iridescent blue-green tūī now, and reached a hand out to catch the white card he had just dropped that matched the tuft of feathers under his chin. She turned the business card over to read it as he returned to his pūriri moth shape— Raven's Haven. She stared blankly at the words.

"What? Isn't this the retirement village for old witches? What's so important about it?"

I don't know. It was pinned to a map of Karori on his wall that had the barrier traced in red thread around it. I still don't know if he's studying it or causing it though. We need to get out of here. I'll meet you back at the flat. I'm going to fly over Wrights Hill reserve on the way back and see if I can sense whatever is anchoring this thing.

"Keep away from the barrier this time. You can't waste your energy testing it like that if I'm still being drained. I'm going to go for a ride and clear my head."

The wind was picking up as Trinity tore down the rest of the hill. She considered cycling through the tunnel just to prove to herself that she could, but she still couldn't stand the thought of leaving Saifa behind even briefly. Instead, she turned left and headed back down the road between the looming pōhutukawa and the fading mural that covered the scungy dark concrete retaining wall that marked this edge of Karori. Another marker of the invisible divide that Saifa could not cross. She needed somewhere she could gather her thoughts. The silence of the dead gathered in the nearby cemetery called to her. The dead were simple, peaceful. Maybe she could find answers in their quiet. She pedalled up the hill as hard as she could, staying in a higher gear just to feel the burn in her legs and lungs.

The entrance to the cemetery was flanked by a fire station and she wondered what exactly they thought the dead got up to. The dead didn't create fire, they succumbed to it. She should know. The dark memories threatened to suck her down into despair and she decided to leave her bike near the main gate and enter on foot. Biking was speed and freedom but sometimes you needed to feel the connection to the bones beneath you through the soles of your feet.

She paused at the black-painted lychgate that led to a field of identical headstones arranged in semi-circles. The sign at the entrance said "Peace with Honour", a war memorial. She had fought a silent war her entire life, set on that path when her affliction first manifested and her grandmother whisked her away from everyone and everything she had ever known. Always staying one step ahead of the invisible threats that would enslave a power source like her without a second thought. She envied the dead their peace with honour. Her war was not about honour, it was about survival. Although she suspected that was the case of all wars when you got down to it. She stepped into the cover of the lychgate and breathed in deep, borrowing some of the dead's peace. They wouldn't miss it.

She sat down on the narrow bench and pushed the noises of the outside world away, the dog barking in the distance, the whirring of a bird startled into flight, the sound of the first drops of rain on the roof tiles above her. As she inhaled again, she felt the weight of the charm dragging on her neck and pulled it over her head to tuck away in her pocket. Her fingers stroked the cold metal of the derailleur as she tried to think through how they were going to get Saifa free and where they would run to when they did. She leaned back against the side of the lychgate and sighed. For a day or two, she'd thought maybe they could stay longer this time. They didn't often find a warm, dry flat when they moved and they certainly didn't find pastries. It wasn't fair. She just wanted to stop moving for a little while. To be present. To call somewhere home.

She caught movement out of the corner of her eye and sat up straighter. The rain was growing heavier, pattering out a rapid staccato beat on the small roof above her.

"Can I share your shelter?" a voice asked.

A man ducked into the lychgate preceded by a large black and tan huntaway dog on a leash. Trinity reached a hand out for the friendly dog to sniff and then raised her eyebrows in surprise as the man pulled the hood of his raincoat back.

"Dante! Hi. I wasn't expecting to see you here."

"I always walk Fern here when it looks like it's going to get muddy on the hill trails. What's your excuse?" he said, sitting down beside her.

Fern's head was firmly ensconced between her knees begging for a scritch. Trinity obliged, ignoring his question. "Her name's Fern? She's gorgeous."

"Short for Inferno," Dante said, reaching over to scratch behind her other ear.

"Ha! Love it." Trinity looked out at the rain that was sending rivulets of water flowing down the road's gutters. She was already starting to shiver from the southerly change and all the blood had left her fingers. It had been warm when she'd left the flat and she wasn't dressed for this. She should have checked the weather forecast.

"Are you riding back?" Dante asked.

"Yeah. I left my bike by the gate."

"My car's just around the corner. I can chuck your bike up on the rack and give you a ride?"

Trinity hesitated, but she had always hated the cold and she'd be an ice cube by the time she rode across the entire suburb in the wind and rain to get home. The first thunks of hail on the roof made her decision for her. "Thanks. That would be awesome."

Dante left her with Fern and ran out into the hail. A few minutes later, he pulled up in a blue Jeep. The hail had let up, but the rain was harder than ever. He let Fern into the back and then held the door open for her as she made a dash for the gate. Her fingers shook with cold as she unlocked her bike and loaded it onto the rack, and then she could finally climb into the haven of the SUV.

"The seats should warm up in a second," Dante said as they pulled out onto the road.

"What happened to the Porsche?" she asked.

"I had to colour-coordinate with Fern's leash," he joked. "The Porsche isn't really dog friendly."

She resisted the urge to ask him how many cars he owned.

"Fancy a hot drink at mine on the way home?" he asked.

Trinity looked down at her sopping wet clothes. "I'm not really in a fit state for social calls," she said.

"Don't be silly. I'll start the fire and you'll be dry in no time."

A fire did sound nice. Dante didn't wait for her reply. He was already pulling off at Homewood Ave and Trinity noticed the houses they were passing seemed to be getting larger and larger. He braked by a high stone wall where a wrought iron gate was opening automatically. She could see a large turning circle in front of what could only be described as a mansion up ahead, but he turned off before they reached it and descended a driveway that curved into a basement car park underneath the majestic house.

"What is it that you do again?" Trinity asked, her eyes slightly wide at the wealth on display.

He flicked her a grin as he got out, clearly not the slightest bit self-conscious. "I'm an investor."

She rolled her eyes. Could he get any vaguer? She meant to ask him what he invested in, but as soon as she shut her car door Fern came racing around to jump up at her, tail wagging furiously.

"Fern! Down girl! Come here!" Dante said, sternly.

Trinity grinned as the dog licked her face and then grabbed her paws to back her up. "She's just excited."

Dante had grabbed a towel and Fern's body wriggled with excitement as he dried her coat and wiped the mud from her paws.

"Shall we go get you warmed up?" he asked, as he stood up.

His blond hair was still dripping from his run through the rain and she itched to reach out and wipe the drop of water that had run down his jaw. Before she realised what he was doing, he'd reached out and grabbed her hand to steer her up to the house. His fingers were blissfully warm on her cold skin, almost too warm.

"You're freezing!" he said, cupping her hand in both of his as they walked and only letting go when they entered the kitchen to put the jug on to boil. "What do you fancy? A hot toddy?"

"Isn't it a little early for that?" Trinity asked.

"No. Hot toddy it is," he said, grabbing two glass mugs and some fresh lemons.

Five minutes later, she was ensconced on a couch that was so soft it felt like it might swallow her, sharing a thick alpaca-fibre blanket with Dante as her numb fingers slowly thawed around her hot drink. For the second time that day, she breathed in the scent of lemon, only this time it was mingled with fiery whiskey and cinnamon in steam that warmed her face as she held the liquid close.

"Feel better?" Dante asked, brushing a stray hair from her face. The presumptuous touch should have annoyed her, but the flicker of loneliness she'd seen in his eyes the other day was there again and she couldn't bring herself to push him away.

"Yeah," she said, and was surprised that it was true. The whiskey was taking the edge off her anxiety and focussing on the warmth returning to her fingers and toes distracted her from thinking about the discomfort of questions she had no answers to. She felt a little fuzzy around the edges, but in a good way. Like the harsh edges of her stress had been sanded away. As she looked around the room, her eyes rested on a portrait of an old lady hanging above the fireplace. The oil paint was cracked in places and the painting felt as old as its subject. "Is she a relative of yours? She looks kind," she said.

Dante looked at the painting and then stared into the fire. She could see the residue of grief in the shadows that crossed his face. "Not by blood. We were family by choice. She left me a precious gift."

Trinity frowned in confusion. The artwork looked at least a hundred years old and the woman's hair was white, her face a map of gentle wrinkles. Dante talked about her as if they'd actually met. Had he paid to make the painting look antique? What a strange way to spend your money. Although it didn't look like he had any shortage of it. She opened her mouth to ask him, but there was something in his posture that made her pause. He looked as vulnerable as she'd ever seen him, lost in memories. She knew all about painful memories. She didn't need to drag him through that.

"What did you put in this? It's delicious," she said, changing the subject.

"Just ridiculously expensive whiskey, fresh lemon, ridiculously expensive manuka honey, and my own top-secret blend of spices," Dante said, returning his attention to her. The arrogance was back, but there was a hint of self-deprecation in his tone as if he knew how she saw him.

Trinity raised an eyebrow at his boasting but her retort drifted away from her as she found herself caught by his eyes again. The intensity of his focus was mesmerising. She looked down at her drink to distract herself and watched the steam drifting upwards from the hot liquid instead. "What kind of spices are we talking?"

Dante laughed. "All legal, I promise. There's a bit of valerian in there. That might be what you're noticing. It relaxes you. You looked stressed. What were you stressed about?"

Trinity took another sip of her drink. "Getting home in the cold."

"Fine. Don't tell me," Dante said, pretending to pout.

Trinity sighed silently. She could tell this guy was trouble. She still didn't feel any sense of power from him, but he was trouble anyway. Dante had resources. The last thing she needed was her magic contaminating him and making him into a stalker with unlimited funds to chase her, no matter how cute and lonely he was. She mentally shook herself. What was wrong with her? She shouldn't be thinking about how cute anyone was. She should be breaking the barrier on the valley and getting the hell out of there.

"I should get home. The rain's eased up." She leaned over him to put her drink on the side table.

"Should you? There's no hurry." He hadn't moved, but his voice had shifted low and suggestive. She was already leaning close and she could feel his breath on her ear. His face was all innocence when she turned towards him but his eyes were focussed on her lips. The ache of loneliness in her chest that was always there just beneath the surface grew sharper. She was so tired of always holding herself apart. She couldn't take what he was offering but maybe she could pretend she was going to a little while longer. Just until the ache was bearable again.

"Yes. I should," she said, standing up before she gave in to the pain and did something she regretted. She could hear her Grandmother's voice echoing from distant memory telling her she would be consumed by her relationships. She could feel the teeth waiting to sink into her flesh.

He walked her back down to the basement to fetch her bike. "Want to hit the trails again this weekend? We could head up Mākara Peak," he said, as she pulled on her helmet.

She looked over at him leaning casually against the wall, all lean muscle and charm, and she couldn't bring herself to turn him down. There was no harm in a bit of mountain biking and with long sleeves and her gloves on there would be no chance of stray contact causing a problem. "Sure."

CHAPTER FIVE

Trinity was worried about Saifa. He'd told her he was being careful not to expend too much energy in his searches but even so, she could tell the power he managed to siphon from her was barely enough to sate him. She could feel his presence shrinking, becoming less substantial. His eyes that usually burned with an internal flame, smouldered like banked coals.

Every day, he flew out in search of whatever was anchoring the net that held him captive. Some days Trinity went too, riding the bush paths on the outskirts of human occupation searching for anything that might give a clue. But mostly he just told her she was holding him up. She wished she could grow wings like he did so she could help more. Instead, she felt chained to her laptop. She'd had a sudden influx of copywriting work and they both knew she had to make money while she could. The last move had emptied her savings and there were no guarantees for freelancers.

Saifa was so tired he didn't even make snide remarks at her as she spread Charlie's business plan out across the coffee table night after night when she'd finished the day's contract work. She'd fallen into a pattern of coffee and breakfast with Charlie every morning but she'd still been avoiding dinner with him. She knew Saifa would tell her to go but it felt wrong to enjoy a dinner when he had to control his own hunger again and again so as not to hurt her.

Dante texted at random times:

Fern misses you, accompanied by a selfie of him and the dog looking sad.

Rode this sweet trail today and thought of you.

Shall we grab dinner after our ride this weekend?

As the week passed, Saifa improved a little. She could sense her power levels increasing and it was almost enough for him. She didn't know if she was adjusting to the extra drain or if whoever had been stealing it had taken a break. She didn't ask what Saifa was preying on when he went hunting.

It was taking a toll on her too, being drained by both their captor and Saifa. Not that she had even felt the former happening. If she did, she might have been able to figure out the mechanism. She could not begrudge Saifa her power after half a lifetime of keeping her safe but when she was curled up in bed at night, the wish that she did not need to be consumed to survive was overwhelming.

She took solace in her mornings with Charlie and then berated herself for doing so. She shouldn't be letting him get close, but that didn't change the fact that every morning she checked the mirror twice before descending to the bistro, and every morning he had something different waiting for her—dark chocolate brownie, moist carrot cake, Devonshire tea with scones piled high with cream and jam.

They left the feed from the cameras in Mr Birdwood Street's house playing on the flat's TV all the time. It was the only lead she could keep an eye on. The only way she could contribute. His name was Reymond Underwood, but they always called him Mr Birdwood Street anyway. No one in their right mind gave their true name away to strangers, so it was as accurate as anything else.

She watched him as he went about his business. The magic he undertook was mundane, just a spell here or there to dehumidify the shaded house or find his car keys, and his hobbies were even more so. Did anyone even watch reality TV anymore? Apparently so. Nothing gave him away as the cause of their captivity and she doubted he was capable of the kind of power it took to cast a barrier around an entire suburb.

On Friday, Saifa fluttered through the window in the late afternoon light and circled her head repeatedly, bashing his wings against her face. *I've found one of the anchors. It's on the communications tower at Mākara Peak. We need to go look.*

"Alright, alright! Get off me. What did you see?"

A ball of razor wire with the binding elements contained within it. I can't make them all out but there is a spirit held there, a sprite I think.

"A captive sprite? Caged in razor wire? That's awful."

Not a captive. A spirit. It's dead. I'm guessing some or all of its remains are anchoring it in the construct.

Trinity's eyes grew wide. "Are you sure? Who would kill a sprite? That's like kicking a kitten."

I am certain.

Trinity was already grabbing her shoes and a headlamp. "Show me."

She rode the four-wheel-drive tracks up to the peak. The light was already fading and she didn't want to waste any time navigating unfamiliar single tracks in the dark. The sky glowed red with the sunset as they reached the peak. Trinity barely took the time to stare out at the expansive views, two coastlines and hillsides covered in slow-turning wind turbines, before circling the wire link fence surrounding the communications tower. She decided to cut herself an entrance that would be hidden by the bush rather than scaling it or breaking the lock. She had a feeling she might need to return and she wanted easy access. The sky was black and the stars were showing their faces by the time she had a hole she could get through.

Saifa had changed to a bat-form again, an extant species this time—the native long-tailed bat. He was hanging upside-down halfway up the communications tower next to one of the satellite dishes, his eyes reflecting the light of her headlamp as she peered upwards.

The anchor is here. I can't fly any higher.

She sighed and stared up into the darkness wondering how she ended up in these situations. Then she grabbed a cold steel bar and started clambering up the tower's ladder, hoping the wind that was pulling at her layers of clothing didn't grow any stronger. It was already making an eerie whistling noise through the structure, or maybe that was the voice of the spirit drifting from its cage.

The light of her headlamp reflected strangely off the crisscrossing metal of the tower and once she was partway up the darkness meant she could no longer tell whether she was one metre or 100 metres from the ground. When she reached Saifa's hanging body, she swung herself carefully out towards the edge of the structure where she could see the anchor lodged behind one of the satellite dishes like a spherical razor wire bird's nest. She braced herself as best she could against the frame so she had one hand free.

The ball of razor wire glowed bright under her headlamp, the cool LEDs making it appear like a blue-white sun complete with shadowy sunspots where the dark magical contents that gave the spell its power lurked. She leaned as close as she dared, trying to identify the objects contained within. Dark red embroidery thread was twisted all through the wire, along with wisps of something she couldn't quite make out. She wished she could climb up here in daylight, but there was no way she could risk being seen.

Someone's coming. Saifa's voice sounded in her mind.

She flicked off her headlamp. In the darkness that

followed, the only sense she had of direction was the cold metal that pressed into her legs until they ached. A dangerous tingle started in her toes as one leg fell asleep. She shifted her weight as best she could and then froze as three mountain bikers passed below her, out for a night ride. She hoped none of them spotted her bike in the scrub. She'd made sure it was off the track, but it would reflect their lights if they looked in that direction and then it would only be a matter of time before they hunted for the "missing" rider. Her right leg started cramping.

She reached a hand out to get a better grip to shift position and bit off a yelp as she misjudged the distance and sliced open a finger on the razor wire. A series of images and sounds flashed in her mind as the metal bit through her skin—a concrete bunker, the lychgate from the cemetery, what looked like a twisted jet-black bonsai pōhutukawa tree with strangely familiar geometric fruits hanging from it, and the sharp teeth of a sprite bared in a final desperate scream that reverberated inside her skull. Her grip slickened as her finger bled and her hand slid on the tower's metal, jerking her consciousness back to the present. She swore silently to herself.

The riders below her had passed and as soon as their lights were out of sight, she flicked hers back on. She managed to re-brace herself and reached into her pocket for one of her gloves. It would catch the blood until she got back down. Once she had it on, she inspected the wire and carefully wiped away any of her blood that she could see from the magical anchor and the tower. The last thing she wanted was to find she'd accidentally given away her identity to its maker. You could do a lot with someone's blood.

Clean-up finished, she took a series of photos of the contraption from as many angles as she could with her phone. She was acutely aware that the longer she stayed up here, the more likely she was to have an accident or be discovered. She just had to hope she could adjust the lighting and zoom on the photos when she got home. Before she started her descent, she pulled at one of the embroidery threads wrapped around the wire until she could use the razors to slice a finger-length of it off, tucking it safely in her pocket. She could feel her blood dripping down her arm from her finger as she made her way back down. She took a closer look once she was safely back on the ground, not too deep. She wrapped a sticking plaster around it from her saddlebag and pulled her gloves back on.

"Ready to go?" she whispered to Saifa.

Yeah. Let's get you home and see what we've got. Are you OK to ride? He sounded worried.

"It's just a scratch. I'll be fine."

It's not like you to be that careless.

"Some of us don't have the benefit of echolocation."

Saifa kept a thread of connection between them as she rode back down the hill to civilisation and she told him about the vision she'd had when she cut herself on the magical anchor.

They must be the other anchor locations. Probably three on the boundaries and a central control point. This body's echo-loca-

tion picked up some of what that ball of razor wire contained. It was hard to decipher because the wire was so tangled, but it definitely contains the remains of a sprite. I think the entire thing is a trap that wraps its prey when sprung.

Trinity shivered at the thought of the sharpened razor wire tightening into a ball around her. The echoes of the sprite's dying scream played in her mind. The sooner they could break whatever spell this was and get out of here, the better. But with that many anchors and death magic involved, she wasn't sure how exactly that was going to happen.

She collapsed into bed as soon as they were home and fell asleep to the feeling of Saifa settling onto her face to siphon her power. It was an indication of just how tired she was that even that didn't keep her awake.

She slept in the next day until the sun was high overhead and glaring into her eyes through the skylight over the bed. She staggered to the bathroom fuzzy-headed and rubbing her eyes. It took two coffees before she could face getting dressed. She checked her phone and groaned as she realised she was supposed to be riding back up to the peak with Dante in a couple of hours and she hadn't got any of her work done last night.

She made herself another coffee and toast and sat down with her computer. Saifa had left her a message typed on her screen: *Afternoon, Sleepyhead. I'm going to check the other locations you saw.* He'd already transferred the image files from the previous night onto the computer. She wondered if he'd stuck with his endemic animals or if he'd caved and given himself hands for the task. The video feed from Mr Birdwood Street's house was still playing on the TV screen. It looked like he was doing a crossword in his lounge. Not exactly a nefarious past-time. She sighed and pulled up the article she was working on. The sooner she started, the sooner it would be done.

By the time she met Dante at the bottom car park of the Mākara Mountain Bike Park, her brain was functioning almost normally. There was no sign of either of his flashy cars, he must have ridden there. He was leaning on the fence by a wooden bridge that would take them over a stream and up into the single tracks.

"Hey! Ready for some fun?"

She stopped next to him and was caught by surprise when he kissed her cheek in greeting, his hand gripping her shoulder gently as he leaned in. She looked down at her hands to cover the flush in her cheeks and adjusted her gloves. Her finger was still sore from the previous night and she'd had to use her spare pair that didn't fit as well while the others dried. The seam was rubbing against her cut.

"Yeah. I'm all set," she said, as she finished shifting the fabric. She avoided making eye contact until he'd stepped back.

"Need some new gloves?" he asked, reaching out to touch the one she'd been adjusting.

"Nah. I just cut myself making dinner last night. Right in the wrong spot."

"Well, in that case you'll have to let me make you dinner

tonight so we can save you from yourself." He had shifted his grip so he was cupping her hand in his, his face hovering close to hers with those mesmerising eyes.

The crunch of gravel of another rider passing by them snapped Trinity back to herself and she rocked back a little on her bike. She couldn't afford any distractions. She needed to be focussed on getting out. "Sorry. I can't tonight. I've got a deadline I need to meet."

"Next time, then," Dante said, fetching his bike from the fence line. She could hear the disappointment hidden in his voice.

In the daylight and riding the more exciting single tracks, Trinity had to admit it would be sad to leave such a stunning park behind. The bush was rich with beautiful native ferns and the screeching calls of kākā echoed across the valley.

There was no one else around when they reached a dizzying swing bridge and Trinity dismounted halfway across to lean over the rail and peer at the drop below, revelling in the sensation of being suspended above the earth away from all the stress and fear that it contained. The gentle breeze and Dante's presence made the whole structure sway in place like a boat becalmed. She could only imagine what it would be like to stand there with the howling gusts the city was known for tearing through the gully.

"Stunning isn't it. Selfie?" Dante said.

Trinity turned around to tell him she didn't do selfies, they left a trail that could be followed, but before she could say anything he had his arm around her and his phone poised ready. She pursed her lips in annoyance as he took the photo.

"Don't go posting that on social media or anything," she said.

"It can be our little secret," he grinned, letting his hand slide down from her shoulders to her waist.

She looked up at him in exasperation, but his smile was infectious and she couldn't help responding. With the warmth of the sun on her face and nothing but fresh air and the sounds of birdsong and rustling leaves surrounding her, she let herself relax for a second and leaned her head on his shoulder. If she had been a normal witch, she would have been able to do this kind of thing without a second thought. How long had it been since she'd really connected with someone? Her string of ill-fated exes had been conveniences to keep loneliness at bay, ironic really given how inconvenient they had become. Dante's hand on her waist tightened, pulling her closer. All she had to do was tilt her face up…

She watched two tūī squabbling in the distance and sighed, pulling away. She needed to get home to Saifa. Her fear for him grew every day and she worried for the day it might become a fear *of* him. She couldn't bear to lose him too.

"How much further to the peak?" she asked, trying not to focus on the feel of Dante's hand drifting across her back as she stepped towards her bike.

"I'll race you," he said.

Trinity jumped on her bike and took off. She couldn't say if she was racing towards the peak or away from the escalating temptation Dante had become. It didn't really matter because within minutes she'd forgotten everything but the rhythm of the pedals and scanning the track for the best line.

The peak arrived too soon. She wished she could just keep going and not look back. She was careful this time to leave more space between the two of them as they stared out at the view she had barely noticed the night before. She didn't want to be caught out again, or at least she wouldn't be caught out again even if she wanted to. Her eyes caught on the communications tower as she turned in place taking in the 360-degree vista. Was it her imagination or could she see a little smear of red on one of the struts? She pulled at the seam of the glove that was making her cut finger sting after the long ride.

"It looks like a giant climbing frame doesn't it?" Dante said, noting the direction she was looking.

Trinity shifted her weight and glanced at him to see if there was anything behind the question, but he was clearly focussed more on her than anything around them. His eyes flicking down to her lips before meeting hers again.

"Or a giant's drumkit," she replied, shifting the conversation away from last night's memories.

Her finger was still aching and she pulled her glove off to check the sticking plaster was still in the right place, shaking her hand as if it might shake the ache away. Dante moved closer and caught it in his, turning it over to inspect where she had bandaged.

"Strange place to cut yourself," he murmured, his fingers gently tracing the bandage on the outside of her pinky finger.

Trinity shrugged and pulled her hand away. "Well, I'm a terrible cook."

"Are you sure I can't make you dinner tonight?" One of his hands was toying absent-mindedly with the pendant he always wore and Trinity found herself wishing he would reach out and take her hand again, wishing she could say yes to dinner.

She pushed his arm playfully, feeling his bicep tense beneath her touch "Stop trying to get me in trouble. I'm on a deadline."

He raised his hands in surrender. "Fine. But I'm definitely taking you out for coffee next week."

CHAPTER SIX

Saifa was waiting for her when she got back to the flat. He'd made himself unnaturally large even for a pūriri moth, his wingspan stretching the length of the coffee table. He did that sometimes when he was grumpy.

Where have you been?

"I went out for a ride. It helps me think better."

I thought letting you sleep in might help you think better. His voice was sullen in her mind.

"What did you find?"

The anchors are where your vision suggested. The Lychgate is in the cemetery, the bunker is part of a historic fortress up on the Southern hills.

Trinity felt a moment of guilt as she realised she hadn't told Saifa that she had been to the Lychgate already. He'd found it anyway, though. Bringing it up now would just make his mood worse.

Did you look at the photos at least?

Trinity blushed with shame and opened the computer to bring them up, playing with the light settings to try and get a better look. "It's difficult to see. There's definitely the remains of a sprite in there like you said, and there's a reflection of some sort of crystal but the glare is too bright to make out the colour, the red thread for control and sacrifice..." She fished the thread she'd clipped from the anchor out of her jacket pocket and placed it on the white glass top of the coffee table. Then she flicked through the photos to see if any had a better angle. "There's something else showing in this one. I think it's a stick and something braided."

Saifa shrunk himself and crawled onto the keyboard for a closer look. *A snare? Or a representation of one at least.*

"That makes sense. Can we break it now?"

I don't know. Sacrificial magic is always tricky to unwind and we still don't know where the control key is. The other three anchors are a classic mind, body, power trinity.

"I assume the one from the peak will be mind, given it has a spirit encased in it. If we can smash one, it may destabilise it enough so we can get out."

Or the power may just rebound at us. It's unusual to spread a net so wide without losing its effectiveness. There's no guarantee breaking the anchor would have any effect if we don't take out the control key for the network.

"The key has to be that black tree from my vision. I guess we need to find that before we do anything."

I've got a better idea. Let's fire a warning shot and see if Mr

Birdwood Street squirms. At least that way we can rule him in or out as the cause.

"And what if we kick that nest and a swarm of wasps comes out?"

Then we'll know we kicked the right one and we can search his house again for the tree.

Trinity rolled her eyes, but she could hear the hint of desperation in his voice. She hadn't noticed before, but his form had gained a slight transparency, like someone was playing with the settings on a photo. The green shades of his wings shifted tone as he moved from the black keys of the keyboard to the white glass of the coffee table. The colours were showing through his body. He was starving himself to keep his oath to her. They needed to figure out who they were facing.

"Alright. Is he home?" She flicked the television to the surveillance feed and watched the figure in the distant house stirring something over the stove.

Maybe if we distract him, his cooking will catch fire, Saifa said, hopefully.

"Given he's probably perfectly innocent that seems a little mean. So, what are we using as a boot? I've got the thread we can use to target the Mākara Peak anchor."

I don't know why you bother with all that symbolism stuff. You don't need it. Let's try and extract that poor sprite's spirit and set it free. That should trigger a reaction.

"Yeah, well. I don't know why you bother with those native animal forms. We all have our eccentricities. Mine help me focus."

I can draw the spirit to another plane, if you can sever the connection to the anchor.

Trinity eyed him warily. "You look pretty hungry. Will you be able to resist a weak meal?"

She knew it was a mistake as soon as she said it. Saifa was tired, desperate and starving. He lost his temper. He shifted form before her in an instant, becoming an absence that sucked all light from the room with two points of fiery swirling maelstroms for eyes. She felt his voice, usually modulated in her mind, as a burning vibration in every bone of her body. *Do. Not. Call. Me. Oathbreaker. Human.*

Trinity couldn't draw breath. Her heart stopped beating for an aching moment. A distant part of her mind compared the sensation to what she had felt when they first met years ago. He hadn't been strong enough to have this effect back then, he'd been a shadow of a shadow. Back then, he had bolstered the natural effects of his presence by twisting and amplifying her fear as he latched on to her to drag the power from every single pore of her body. Their bargain had been born of her desperation to survive and sealed with a shared oath—she would feed him her excess power every day so he need never be hungry while she lived, and he would cease preying on her kind and any of the other intelligent creatures that travelled between planes. The witch whose scream for help she had answered, the witch she had saved by intervening, had fled as soon as Saifa had turned his attention to her.

Trinity wrestled her eyelids closed against the terror of his form and when she opened them again Saifa was a delicate moth once more, perched on the breakfast bar with his tiny antennae thrumming. She took a gasping breath.

"Don't get your wings in a twist. A simple 'yes' would have sufficed," she croaked.

He didn't deign that with a response, but she could feel the tension had left the room.

I will fly up to the anchor and work from there, he said, taking off out the window without waiting for a reply.

Conscious of his criticism of her methods, she didn't grab as many of the focus objects as she might usually. She'd been using them like mnemonics, but she had been relying a little too heavily on them in the last year or two. Instead, she put her charm to hide any trace of herself around her neck and picked up only the red thread that was the connection she needed to the anchor, letting it rest in the palm of her hand as she stared at one of the photos on the screen until she could hold the image of the anchor in her mind's eye.

She closed her eyes and focussed on the anchor, the feeling of being suspended on the tower buffeted by the winds, the light starting to fade, the subtle smell of the clay dirt that formed the tracks below. She felt the tenuous connection from the thread in her hand stretch out towards the peak and she sent her consciousness along it like a zipline. She could only see Saifa's true form on this plane. His presence felt just as terrifying as it had in the flat, but the physical distance between them lessened the more unpleasant side effects. She reminded herself to breathe, dragging air into her lungs until her body remembered that it could. She focussed on the ball of razor wire and the beating golden spirit she could now see within it. She avoided looking at Saifa's eyes. Otherwise, the maelstrom of power that they were a window to would suck her in whether he wanted to or not.

Saifa's focus was on that shining golden spirit and she could see it straining towards him, unable to resist the insatiable black-hole of his true nature. Constrained by the anchor that was its cage, the spirit looked wrong. It oozed closer to him where it should have floated like a tiny incandescent star. As it started to surge against the outer circumference of the anchor, she saw that its golden light was streaked with dark brown as if parts of its essence had died and scabbed over.

Saifa hissed in anger and she felt the pull of his power even stronger. Her hand gripped the arm of the couch hard as she fought to keep her balance and avoid being drawn in. Agonisingly slowly, the spirit bulged outwards through a gap in the razor wire like an incorporeal hernia. When only the last fragment of dirty brown essence was hooked around the wire, Saifa's voice rang in her mind. *Cut it now! I can't hold it much longer.*

Trinity's hand spasmed closed around the red embroidery thread and she shoved all of her power down the connection to the anchor, imagining it as a burning scalpel that scraped down the curved invisible edge of the razor wire ball like she was a barber giving the face of magical entrapment a close shave. It should have been well within her normal oversupply of power to sever the connection, but as depleted as she was it took everything she had and left her with the kind of ache that fills your lungs when you keep exhaling even when there is no air left. A keening screech filled her mind as the golden spirit shot free, the sound immediately cut short as the limply glowing ball disappeared into another plane, dragged by Saifa's power. She took comfort from the fact that only traces of dull-brown remained in the anchor. She had not severed the spirit in two.

Trinity gathered herself to check on Saifa but before she could, she was shocked back into her own body by a sharp jolt as the couch jumped underneath her and every glass and plate in her kitchen clattered in place. Disoriented from the sudden shift of perspective, she had barely registered that it was an earthquake and not her dizziness that was making the room spin before the movement subsided to a gentle rocking.

She was still swaying in place when Saifa reappeared, less substantial than ever. *Did he react?*

Trinity was so distracted by everything that had happened she'd forgotten the point was to see what Mr Birdwood Street would do. She rewound the surveillance footage and played it back, keeping an eye on the time stamp. He showed no sign of reaction until the lampshade started swaying from the earthquake.

"Hard to tell. If the sprite's spirit set off the earthquake, he could be reacting to either."

That wasn't the sprite, it was the anchor itself. I don't know how he connected it so deep in the earth but it explains how he made the barrier so large.

Trinity looked up the details of the earthquake online. "Six kilometres deep. Magnitude 3.7. Epicentre here, obviously. 5:17 pm."

She checked the timestamp on the recording again. Mr Birdwood Street definitely hadn't moved before the physical signs of the earthquake at 5:17. She fast-forwarded to real-time and watched as he hunched over a bowl of water in his kitchen.

He's trying to locate the source of the earthquake.

"That doesn't mean anything. Any witches in the area would be. You could feel the power dragging those seismic waves. Actually, that's a point, the release of power from the sprite would have preceded the earthquake by a few seconds at least. We should have seen some reaction from him earlier."

So we still have nothing. Saifa sighed.

A rapping sound on the door to the flat jerked her out of her thoughts.

It's Charlie, Saifa said as she jumped to her feet.

Her heart sank. "Could it have been him?"

Don't be silly. I'd know if he had that kind of power. I'm going to go find something to eat. You should do the same with him.

The knock sounded at the door again as Saifa flitted out the window. She glanced one more time at Mr Birdwood Street and then turned the television off. Her phone buzzed as she checked her reflection in the mirror on the way to opening the door. She looked pale, but there was no other obvious sign that she'd been working magic to release the spirit of a murdered sprite from the horrifying confines of the anchor suspended on a communications tower in the distance. She tucked her charm pendant in the side-table draw and checked her phone.

Are you OK? That was a sharp one. The text was from Dante.

She flicked him a thumbs up and then turned notifications off.

Charlie's hand was raised to knock again as she pulled the door open and she could see the relief spread across his face when he saw her. "Are you okay? Did anything fall?"

"Yeah, I'm fine. Just some rattling crockery. Is the bistro intact? Shouldn't you be with your customers?"

"No customers tonight. It's been really quiet. Just one smashed wine bottle that was too close to the edge of the shelf," he said.

She felt guilty as she heard the hint of stress in his voice when he mentioned having no customers. She'd happily eaten his baking every morning without ever really thinking about how few people she'd been seeing downstairs as she came and went. She needed to make more progress on helping him before she had to leave.

"Well. I can be your customer for the evening. I'm starving and I can't cook to save myself," she said with a smile.

"I was actually thinking I might take advantage of the excuse to close early," he said.

Her smile slipped. "Oh. Of course. No need to stay open just for me."

"But I've got fresh-made gluten-free bread I was hoping to test on you that won't keep and an open bottle of Otago Pinot I could bring up," he offered.

Trinity felt guilty all over again. Had he been baking gluten-free bread every day just in case she came down for dinner? She stared at her kitchen cupboards trying to remember what she'd bought at the supermarket. "Would it be sacrilege to eat that with peanut butter and drink the wine from a mug?" she asked.

Charlie laughed and rolled his eyes. "Yes. Yes, it would. I'll bring some French cheese and homemade pesto as well. And I'm sure I can rustle up a wineglass."

Trinity made a show of looking thoughtful. "I don't know. I'll probably cut the cheese all wrong. I might still need some help."

"Two wine glasses then," Charlie said with a smile.

While he went to fetch the food, Trinity cleared the flat. She closed all the images on her laptop and tucked it away, made sure the spy-cam footage wouldn't show up on the television if it was turned on, and hid anything that could possibly be construed as witchy paraphernalia. She was feeling pretty on top of things until she realised her sink was full of dirty dishes, her bed was a tangle of blankets, and she'd forgotten to pick a pair of underwear up off the ground that morning. Five frantic minutes later she was slightly out of breath, the dishwasher was full to overflowing, and her cupboards and drawers were filled with a random assortment of things she'd found on the floor. It was beyond her how there were so many things to pick up when she hardly owned anything.

Charlie's soft tap on the door sounded shortly after and she scanned the room one more time as she went to open it. Her eyes lit on the business card they'd found at Mr Birdwood Street's house and she tucked the card in her pocket.

When she opened the door, Charlie was standing with a colourful blanket folded over one arm like a maître d's napkin. His other hand was holding a large cane basket with the top of a wine bottle poking out the side of its lid.

"I couldn't carry it all and I figured as long as I was putting it in a basket anyway, we could have a picnic," he explained.

"Perfect," she said, stepping aside to let him through the door.

He's your landlord, not your friend, she reminded herself on repeat as she pushed the coffee table to the edge of the room to make space for the picnic blanket. How long had it been since she had a picnic? Not since her grandma was alive. He must have warmed the bread when he was downstairs because she could smell the delicious scent of the yeast blending with the aroma of the thyme embedded in its crust. Their hands brushed as he passed her a glass of wine and they shared a smile.

"To unexpected earthquake picnics," Charlie said, raising his glass in a toast.

The wine tasted of rich fruit and its bouquet hinted at the same herbal smell that was wafting from the bread.

Charlie watched her savouring it. "After offering to drink it from a mug I thought you might be a complete heathen and not appreciate it, but you look like you've just got into the catnip," he joked. "This vintage is famous for its undertones of dried thyme. I like to think of it as the bistro's mascot."

"The bistro name is brilliant. I do love a good pun, and a good Time Lord!"

"Coming from a writer, that is high praise. I can't claim any other talent with words."

"That's just as well. If you were as good with words as you are with flavours I don't think I could take the competition. I don't know why you don't have people flocking here."

Charlie was leaning on his side with his legs stretched out and he rested his head on his hand as he answered. He looked tired, or defeated maybe. "My brother tried to tell me this section was too far out of the way. No one comes into the depths of Karori for a meal, even the people who live here. It doesn't matter how good the food is, if you're spending good money on a gourmet meal people want to go somewhere more exciting than their doorstep. And I'm too far from all the flash houses to get any rich foot traffic."

"Can you diversify? I used to try and make a living off stories and book reviews, but it's marketing copy that pays the bills."

"Maybe. But this is my dream, you know? The food has

to be great, but the atmosphere and the sense of *this* place need to be there, too. That's why the interior downstairs was so important to me. It needs to feel special. It needs that touch of magic. I don't want to mass-produce crab cakes to send off to bland corporate functions. I want to immerse people in an experience. I want them to be able to see the connection between what they're eating, the hands that made it, and the local suppliers that it came from. Fresh meat from the Gipps Street Butchery, cheeses imported by Gamboni's deli, Penny's wonderful preserves... Sorry. I go on a bit if you get me started," his voice trailed off and she could see his cheeks flush red as she reached out to take an olive from one of the bowls on the blanket.

"Don't be sorry. That is a beautiful dream. I'm sure you'll find a way to make it work."

"Do you still write any stories?"

"Not for a long time. I... I move a lot and I just haven't had the energy."

"Why not stay put then? It seems like you can work from anywhere," he said.

Trinity flushed in shame, but it wasn't like she was going to have a relationship with Charlie, anyway. What did it matter if she told him? Maybe it would put him off and he would stop being so distracting. "I have a talent for poor choice in men. It's usually easiest to move."

Charlie burst out laughing and then trailed off when he realised she was serious. "Really? That is so sad. You shouldn't have to leave your home because someone else is an arsehole."

Trinity smiled sadly and shrugged. It was almost sweet that he thought somewhere that she lived might be "home".

"Well, speaking purely from self-interest, I hope you haven't found your latest sorry excuse for a man yet because I need my number one gluten-free taste-tester to stick around. What's more important, scones or men?"

"I assure you, I take my tasting position very seriously. I am completely dedicated to the cause," she joked, taking another slice of bread and wiping every last drop of pesto from the dish before piling a giant wedge of cheese on top. The bread was the perfect mix of satisfying crunchy crust and fluffy middle. It had a slightly nutty taste that perfectly complemented the tang of the soft cheese and the flavours of the pesto.

Later that night as she removed the excess dishes she'd hidden in the dishwasher so she could run it, she wondered if any of her old stories were still on her laptop. She poured herself the last of the wine and sat down to check. In the depths of her writing folder, she found a plan for a novel she'd forgotten she'd even thought of. As she read over the plot points and half-sketched characters, she felt a wave of sadness that she had lost the ability to think like this. She found a link to images she'd saved as inspiration and scrolled through fantasy scenes and objects that she could no longer remember the relationship between. A particular setting caught her eye and she left it open as she flicked back to one of the scenes she'd planned out. Maybe she'd just make a note of that in case she came back to it one day, she thought. Her hands paused and then she opened a new document and started to type. The clattering of fingers to keys didn't stop until the dishwasher beeping broke her concentration an hour and a half later.

Feel better? Saifa asked emerging from behind a blind.

"Geez. How long have you been there?"

Long enough to watch you clean up after what looked like a delightful picnic and write something you actually cared about.

"Stalker."

I am not. May I remind you that I have an impeccable record in ridding you of unwanted attention. I was simply giving you some privacy at a time that looked suspiciously like you might be getting a life.

"Does that mean you're going to change into something less mothy now?"

Are you going to make an actual friend?

"No. I'm going to figure out a way to get you free and get out of here before whoever it is tries to capture me as well."

Saifa was silent as she got ready for bed. His reply was a whisper in her dreams as she drifted off to sleep. *I'm sorry that you have to stay for me. And I'm even sorrier that you'll have to leave. You deserve a place to call home.*

CHAPTER SEVEN

Saifa had perched himself on the side of a kitchen cupboard to watch Trinity finish the rest of the dishes the next morning. She'd told Charlie to leave them and now she was regretting it. She was irrationally scared of breaking anything so she was washing everything by hand.

"You know, if you changed form to something with hands you could dry these for me," she muttered. Her head was aching from too much wine.

It's character building. Besides, I need my rest after a hard night.

Trinity rolled her eyes and held a glass up to check it was spotless. "Don't go full demon on me again, but what *are* you finding to hunt that isn't a person, human or otherwise?" she asked.

The barrier that is trapping me is indiscriminate. It is trapping anything that stumbles here from another plane and they're not all intelligent. And before you ask, I go out of my way to find predators. I know you're a soft touch for magical fauna.

"I'm surprised no one has noticed the influx. What kind of predators are wandering around?"

Not many and they're canny enough to stay hidden in the bush preying on the occasional mountain biker or runner. I found a hellhound. It was tasty enough. Not as delicious as something intelligent, though. You've spoiled me. Hopes and fears add a complexity to your power that an animal cannot match.

Trinity stared down at her hands in the water watching the ripples spreading from them and tried not to think about the question of what Saifa would do when she died and his oath to her was broken. She opened her mouth to change the subject to something safer and then paused, distracted by the way the ripples in the water dispersed as they moved further from her hand.

"Do you think we could adjust the scrying set-up to trace the waves of power from last night?" she said.

Saifa ruffled his wings, stretching them wide before settling back on the cupboard. *Yes. I think so. You want to trace them? We already know the anchor is the origin.*

"Yes. But if we shove the other two anchors in the same way, we should be able to triangulate the waves of power to find a rough location for the key."

That might work. If we're quick, we might be able to catch the echoes from last night. And we can have the spell set up ready to act like a seismometer for the next two. We'd need to figure out what's linking them so deep into the earth to calibrate the rig, though.

Trinity grabbed her computer and sat down to run a search. "You just reminded me, I was meaning to look into why that snare you saw in the anchor was so low-tech. Razor wire and silk embroidery thread are so modern and flashy. The stick and twine were totally out of place. Like if I'd suddenly started using road bike parts as my focus."

Or even worse, an electric-assist, Saifa teased.

Trinity poked her tongue out at him and turned back to the computer. It was embarrassingly quick to find the answer from a simple search of 'snare' and 'Karori'. "Aha! Apparently, the true name of Karori is Te Kaha o nga Rore, 'the ridge for snaring birds'. The name has been so twisted, they must have managed to twist its power as well."

Well. That puts a different spin on things. Even together, we're not going to be able to break the power of the land itself. Very cunning. It won't leave the same signature as human magic, either. Much easier to hide.

"You almost sound like you've got a crush on whoever built it. This is not good news," Trinity said.

You're always so negative. I said we're not going to be able to break the anchors' power. I didn't say anything about the person who built them. This is an opportunity. Imagine what you could do with this kind of network.

"Other than trap you here forever? I literally have no idea."

Sometimes I wonder why I bound myself to you. Hurry up and get your magic toys out before the echoes fade and we have to start again.

Trinity glared at him but went to get the things they

needed anyway. "It's not my fault I didn't grow up with any magical education. I was too busy learning how to hide from everyone and moving town every five minutes. Tell me what you can do with a network like that."

Saifa made a very un-mothlike snort of disgust. He'd never had any patience for her feeling sorry for herself. He did relent and explain as she set up the touchscreen and equipment, though. *If you control the key, you can link any spell you like to it and it will be both amplified and hidden. The witch is using it to trap me, but they are almost certainly also using it to conceal themselves and their power or I'm sure I would have come across them in my searching.*

"So, why is that an opportunity? It sounds like we're doomed."

At that point, Saifa sounded so frustrated with her failure to get the point that he enunciated every word as if she were a three-year-old. *Oh, I don't know. Who could you possibly have to hide from? I'm sure you couldn't find any use for a network where the very land itself would keep you hidden and safe forever.*

"Oh," Trinity said, staring at him in surprise.

She had picked up the cord suspending the disk brake to scry with and it now swung forgotten in her hand. The weight of Saifa's body landing on the contraption snapped her attention back to the task at hand, but her thoughts continued whirling in the background as she went through the familiar motions of the spell and wrapped the red thread from the anchor around the brass of the map pointer. Could she really use this network to protect herself here? The thought made her smile. All her life she had longed to be still. All her life she had longed for a home.

Saifa's voice, still grumpy, cut through her reflection. *Pay attention.*

She hooked the pointer onto the rig and closed her eyes to immerse herself in the memory of the previous night's power surge, directing her own power down to him. She felt Saifa's energy as heat growing beneath her hands, wrapping around her power and shaping it. He fed on magic and he could draw it to him. She knew he was far older than a human could hope to live and his precision was a constant source of awe to her. The way he could control every part of his essence to mould it to what they needed. She could feel the pressure change in the air as his focus shifted from pulling her power into him to pulling the last echoes of ricocheting waves from last night.

Her eyes peeked open as she felt the weight of the make-shift pendulum swinging in her hand. The tip of the map pointer traced out waving lines of energy spreading from the origin point of the anchor at Mākara Peak. When it was complete, the edge of every wave sheared off at the irregular boundary outline of the suburb. It was eerie to see the invisible cage set out so clearly on the map. On their own, these lines gave no clue to where the key might be. But once they'd mapped the other two anchors there should be a visible nexus. Hopefully. Otherwise, they were screwed.

Looks about right, Saifa said.

"Let's just hope we don't shake the whole suburb apart getting the other readings."

I want to check all of the anchors again before we mess with the next one. I think the spirit was just energy needed for establishing the network and to help it function across planes, but I need to check we didn't de-stabilise anything.

"Be careful."

Always. If it's all stable, I'll aim to be at the Lychgate in a couple of hours. You'll need to be here to work the scrying rig.

"Will it work without you here as a focus?"

You'll be catching the bow-wave, not the echo, this time. Just channel it into the rig and it should be fine.

"What will you do to the anchor? Is there another spirit in there?"

No. It's tied into the bodies in the cemetery, knotted really. The threads are tangled in all directions. If we slice one, it should release a small wave. Not enough to rupture a faultline but large enough to register the pattern.

"OK. Just signal me when you're ready."

Saifa paused and inspected her. *You look like shit. You should go out and get some fresh air while you wait.*

Trinity rolled her eyes but he'd already flown out the window before she could come up with a suitably sarcastic response. She caught a flash of red from the underside of his wings as he transformed into a kākā mid-flight. She sat staring at the patterns on the map a while longer before tossing the screen onto the other side of the couch. It wasn't going to become any clearer until they had more data. She scrounged two painkillers from a drawer for her headache and jumped in the shower. By the time she got out, she felt a little more in control.

A message was waiting on her phone from Dante: *Coffee?*

Coffee was exactly what she needed to drive away the last spikes of pain in the base of her neck and she could get some fresh air at the same time. *Sure*, she replied.

I'll pick you up in fifteen.

Trinity swore under her breath about arrogant men who thought you would drop everything to come meet them right away, and then texted him to say she'd meet him on the main road. She didn't like people knowing where she lived. She'd barely been waiting a minute when the metallic green Porsche pulled up next to her and Dante got out. He was back in his tailored white shirt and suit pants, no hint of the daredevil mountain-biker she'd seen on their last two rides.

He kissed her cheek in greeting and opened the passenger door for her. "It's such a nice day, I thought we could go find somewhere scenic," he said.

She tilted her head to the side and watched him looking so sure of himself as she tried to figure out whether he was planning coffee or something else. "OK. I need to be back in an hour though. I have work to do."

The rich smell of coffee filled the car as she got in and she saw two takeaway cups sitting in the cupholders. He didn't drive them far. Just back up to the look-out point they had ridden to on the day they met. They sat on the low wooden fence and drank their coffee staring out across the hills towards the shining waters of the harbour.

"I don't think I'll ever get tired of this view. Wellington can be so beautiful when it's not trying to blow you off a hillside," Trinity said.

Dante shifted position so he was straddling the fence and facing her instead of the view. His left leg was just brushing her back and his right knee rested against hers. "And when it's not trying to shake you off a hillside. Did anything at your place break last night?" he asked.

"Just one of Charlie's wine bottles."

"Who's Charlie?"

Trinity thought about explaining the bistro, but she never gave away her address if she didn't have to. It wasn't worth the risk. "He's my landlord."

"And you have his wine at your place?"

"He's a chef. He brings me food sometimes. He brought dinner last night." She wondered why she felt guilty at the admission.

"What a nice guy," Dante said.

Was it her imagination or had a slight chill crept into his voice? She turned to search his face for any sign of jealousy, but he was distracted by something in the distance.

"Look. Two kererū," he said, his arm brushing past her to point at the sky to her left.

She turned away from him to look where he was gesturing. She could just hear the whooshing of the fat wood pigeons' wings as they tore through the air in the distance. Dante had scooted closer when he reached out and she could feel his body pressed against her back as she watched the birds. When he dropped his hand back down, he left it resting gently on her leg.

Trinity ignored the tired memory of her Grandma's voice in the back of her mind telling her that her relationships would consume her. You couldn't go through life without any contact. She should know, she'd tried. And at least he wasn't her landlord. Sometimes she needed to forget about magic and the people that would hunt her down for her power and just *exist* for a minute. She relaxed back into the warmth of his body and let his arm snake around her waist to pull her closer.

"So, if you're accepting dinner from your landlord, there's no excuse to keep avoiding dinner with me," he said. His voice was low and soft and his lips were brushing against her ear as he spoke.

"I guess I could make some time for you. Not tonight, though," she teased.

"This Friday. My place. Be there by five."

She twisted around to face him again, one eyebrow raised. "Was that a request? I missed the question."

He put down his coffee and cupped the back of her head with his hand, pulling her closer to kiss her softly. "Please?" he asked.

"Well, if you put it that way..."

The sound of his phone ringing broke the moment and he let her go to check who it was. "Sorry, I need to take this," he said, standing up and walking just out of hearing distance before answering it.

Trinity picked up their coffee cups and dropped them in the bin while she waited. Then she watched him leaning nonchalantly on his car as his free hand gestured expansively to make some, no doubt very important point. What did he invest in? He didn't seem like he spent much time working.

She drifted closer and tried to eavesdrop but he was mostly listening now. All she caught was a stray reference to old ladies. Maybe it wasn't a work call after all. She'd returned to bird-watching by the time he finished the five-minute call. "Sorry about that. I need to go take care of something," he said, as he came and wrapped his arms around her again.

"No worries. I've got some work I should be doing anyway. Oh, and I'm coeliac by the way. If you poison me with gluten at dinner I'll never forgive you."

"Really? I have a wheat allergy so it won't be a problem. It's almost like we're made for each other."

He leaned down to kiss her again, but she smiled and shifted away. "Laying it on a bit thick there, sweetheart," she said.

He laughed and pulled her closer again without trying to kiss her this time. "Sorry, I can't help it with you. I promise I'll behave."

There was something intoxicating about his presence and she pressed close to him despite herself, feeling every point where their bodies touched. She rested her head on his chest and felt the edges of his pendant pressing against her cheek from under his shirt. Her mind drifted even as his hands drifted down her back leaving a tingling trail in their wake. It was Dante that pulled away first with a groan. "That call was terrible timing. Hold that thought until Friday?"

She blinked a little as she came out of her daze and smiled as she shook her head at his persistence. "Maybe," she said as she walked back to the car.

They'd stayed out a little longer than she thought and she felt the first tingling of connection with Saifa in her mind as she headed up the stairs to the flat after leaving Dante back at the main road. He'd looked a little hurt when she hadn't let him drop her home.

The network still seems stable. I'm all set. Are you ready?

I just got home. Give me five to set everything up, she sent back.

She only needed three in the end, and by the time she was sending her consciousness down the link between them, she had sunk into a familiar focussed state, her mind empty and calm. The process was similar to the previous night but with so many more points of connection into the anchor from the bodies in the cemetery, Saifa didn't need to use so much energy to draw one out. The only difference this time was that Trinity was trying to do two things at once—holding the scrying apparatus, physically and with her power, while also shaping the blade of energy that would sever the link between the anchor and whichever hapless cadaver from the cemetery Saifa had randomly selected to set free.

Perhaps it was that split in her attention, that distraction, that caught her out. As her power wended with the flames of Saifa's energy in a fiery burst and the images of the skeletons linked to the anchor flickered in a rotating parade before her eyes, she found herself caught in another memory of flames and bodies. She was barely aware of the earthquake rocking the flat and the pointers tracing their patterns on the map sitting in her lap. Instead, images from years past played through her mind.

Saifa had been away when they attacked. He used to disappear for a few days at a time before it was just the two of them. Before the fire. The attackers had surrounded the house bus that was home to her and her Grandmother and charged inside. They had come seeking power and they didn't give a crap about the girl barely out of adolescence in which it resided. They certainly didn't care about the elderly woman throwing herself between them to protect her. Her Grandma hadn't lasted more than a second against them, at least Trinity hoped she hadn't. She hadn't been able to check. Her Grandma's body had crumpled to the ground, revealing a hooded attacker whose face glowed eerily in the light of the blade they wielded before them.

She had panicked, throwing out a hand in self-defence and scattering the power they craved amongst them like a tsunami of fire to shove them all away, too much power. Saifa had been gone too long and it had become unstable. The walls of the bus had glowed red hot. The pot of geraniums on their tiny Formica dining table had shattered. The blast of heat felt as though it was from a demon plane itself.

Saifa had arrived then, drawn by the release of her power. Too late. It was the chaotic maelstrom of his eyes that had pulled her from the wreckage. It was the soft wings of his giant Haast eagle shape that had screened the twisted burned bones of her attackers from her view as he wrapped around her. She had hugged her knees tight to her chest rocking on the damp grass and when he finally let her go, the bodies had disappeared. All except for her Grandmother's, as if he'd known she would need to say goodbye.

She didn't realise she was clinging to herself in that same foetal position on the couch, safe in Karori, until Saifa returned from the Lychgate anchor.

You're safe, dear heart. It's OK. It's over, he said, and the kindness in his voice was enough to make her sit up a little. He didn't talk like that often.

"Sorry. I just... The fire and the bodies. It felt so much like that night."

He changed himself into the large eagle again, the shape he only used when she needed protecting, and she nestled in against the feathers of his chest while he ran his beak through her hair.

It's OK, he repeated, *I won't let that happen ever again.*

Trinity hadn't been lying when she'd told Dante she had work to get done. The whole waiting for someone who'd trapped them to attack you thing was really killing her productivity. Despite the afternoon's magical antics leaving her feeling like she'd just ridden an endurance race, she hauled out her computer and forced herself to sit in front of it until her fingers started making words with the keys. Progress was achingly slow and she blinked in a half-daze when she finally looked up from the screen to realise the living room was dark and night had well fallen outside. She stood to stretch her aching neck and shoulders.

It's about time you took a break, Saifa said, his moth eyes glowing like tiny points of molten lava.

Trinity glanced over at the microwave clock—10:30 p.m. "No wonder I'm starving," she said as her stomach growled embarrassingly loud in the silence.

She had just flicked the lights on to find something to eat when the sound of smashing glass drifted up from the street through the open window. She could see Saifa's shape blurring into a Haast Eagle again from the corner of her vision as she ran to the door. They both remembered the last time someone had broken a window to get into their flat, and no one had been holding them magically hostage back then. This felt far more dangerous.

Let me go first, he said.

"Not like that. What if someone sees you?"

Fine, he said, changing back into his moth form.

Trinity opened the door as quietly as she could and let him flit ahead before slipping down the stairs towards the locked bookcase door. The deadbolt was still holding it firmly closed and she couldn't hear anyone trying to open it from the other side. If they were coming for her, they hadn't figured out where the door was yet.

She tried to gather her power to protect herself and was alarmed at how drained she was. Dealing with the anchor had been exhausting, but she hadn't thought it would take so much. She may as well be a non-witch for all the good it was going to do her tonight.

I can't feel anyone on the other side of the door. Open it, Saifa said.

Trinity twisted the deadbolt and eased the door open, every sense alert for an attack. The bistro was just as quiet as her flat had been. She couldn't leave Saifa to face whoever it was alone. She edged out behind him into the restaurant. The light from the streetlamps was filtered in stripes along the floor by the slatted windows. Her eyes peered into the shadowy corners for any sign of movement, but there was none.

Saifa had flown through the door into the kitchen space and his voice sounded in her mind as she moved towards the other room.

Someone's smashed the glass door to the kitchen with a brick. There's no sign of anyone here.

Trinity sighed. "Kids? It seems unlikely."

There's a smell of something here. A hint of magic. But I can't get a lock on it to trace it.

"Crap. I guess I could call the police..."

Or you could just go upstairs, barricade the door, and pretend you slept through it. Night-time is not when you want to be letting strangers into your house when you know someone is out to get you.

Trinity sighed and headed back upstairs. She almost wished someone had attacked. Anything would be better than waiting for the axe to fall.

We need to triangulate that third anchor before anyone else comes visiting, Saifa said, echoing the urgency she felt.

"Tomorrow," Trinity promised, climbing back into bed.

Charlie's knock on the door came too early the next morning when he arrived to start baking the day's bistro offerings. She blinked sleep from her eyes as he told her about the broken door and asked if she'd heard anything. She was grateful for the fuzz filling her brain that made it easy to act confused.

"I'm so sorry. I must have slept through it."

She told the same story to the cops when they arrived half an hour later. By that time, she'd had a shower and was sitting downstairs with Charlie. He'd been shell-shocked enough that he'd let her take charge of the coffee machine to make them both a cup.

Looking at the blank expression on his face, she went to make them another flat white after the police had left, triple-shot this time. There wasn't much the investigators could go on. There were no signs of theft and it looked like nothing more than an act of vandalism to them. She knew someone had been in the building, but there was no way she could tell the police that and they didn't bother taking any fingerprints. The neighbours were no help. They'd heard the noise but hadn't bothered getting out of bed. She felt sick with guilt. They'd almost certainly been targeting her and it was Charlie that would have to foot the bill.

Charlie half-heartedly took a sip of coffee when she put it down in front of him. "This is actually pretty good. I might offer you a job if I ever get enough customers to justify staff," he said.

"Courtesy of a misspent summer as a barista in my youth," she said, trying to keep her voice upbeat despite the defeatist tone she could hear in his.

Charlie gripped the handle of the cup and twisted it back and forth on the saucer. "I just feel like maybe the universe is trying to tell me this isn't meant to be, you know?" he said.

"No. I don't. Don't let some arsehole with a brick steal your dreams from you."

He smiled a little, but it didn't light up his face in the way it usually would.

"Come on. You can make us some cheese scones dripping with butter while I clean up the mess." When he didn't immediately stand up with her, Trinity grabbed his hand and pulled him up out of his seat. He still looked like a marionette whose strings had been cut. She grabbed a jar from the counter and held it out to him. "Would you like a jelly baby?" she said, in her best Doctor Who impression.

That got a laugh from him. "Alright. Alright. I'm going," he took a jelly baby and squeezed her hand that was still holding his before heading to the kitchen.

Trinity found a brush and shovel under the counter and followed behind him to start clearing the crumbled safety glass from the floor. By the time she'd finished sweeping and taped plastic over the hole, the smell of butter and cheese from the oven had filled the kitchen. The two of them worked around each other in perfect unison like two wheels of the same bike. Trinity took charge of the espresso machine one more time and placed the two cups on the table just as Charlie emerged with a golden steaming scone for each of them. They sat next to each other in the booth seat, looking out at the rest of the bistro from their corner perch.

"To jelly babies," Charlie said, holding out his scone.

"And holding tight to your dreams," Trinity said, tapping her own scone against his and taking a large bite.

"So, who's your favourite Doctor?" Charlie asked.

They sat chatting Doctor Who long past the time when

there was nothing but crumbs and dried milk foam to show for their morning meal. The first inkling Trinity had that something was wrong was losing the thread of the conversation as a sensation of spacey disconnection descended on her brain, followed by crushing fatigue. She didn't realise what was happening at first, putting it down to the stressful morning. The familiar wave of nausea caught her by surprise, as did the angry sense of betrayal. She mumbled an excuse about forgetting a conference call and rushed upstairs to the flat. She was retching as she reached for the bathroom door handle.

Saifa's voice grated in her despairing mind as she heaved over the toilet. *What happened? Gluten?*

"Obviously," she snapped back at him.

Shit. I thought Charlie understood. Was it contamination or did he use the wrong flour?

Wracking pain shot through her torso and tears leaked from her eyes as she heaved. "Way worse than contamination," she groaned.

She couldn't believe she'd become so complacent. A month ago she never would have eaten anything Saifa hadn't checked for her. She shouldn't have trusted Charlie, especially when he was so distracted by the break-in. She'd been so enamoured with being able to eat all the things she couldn't usually have that she'd abandoned all common sense. She should have known better.

Doubled over in pain, the emotional effects reverberated against waves of nausea. She alternated between berating herself and despairing over how she could tell

Charlie. The tears started again, squeezed from her eyes by the violence of her body's heaving to drop onto the tiled floor between feet that shook with cold as her temperature plummeted.

Hours later, when there was nothing left in her stomach, she staggered to the kitchen for a sip of water. "I can't help with the anchor today," she croaked at Saifa.

I know. It can wait. Do you need me to stay here with you?

"I'll be OK," she said, even though she didn't believe it.

There's a stretch of possible locations on the map from the first two results. I'll go scout and see what I can find, he said.

Trinity opened her mouth to reply and then winced and clutched her abdomen as pain shot through her again. She ran back to the bathroom.

Breathe through it, my dear. It won't last forever, Saifa said as he left through the window.

Trinity held tight to her uncharitable thoughts in response rather than send them racing after him. Easy for him to say that it wouldn't last forever. It would last long enough. This was shaping up to be days of illness and probably another month of anxiety and side effects. The timing was suspicious on the back of the break-in. There was no point lashing out at Saifa, though. It was her own stupid fault for trusting someone.

Saifa spent most of the next few days winging over Karori searching for any hint of power that would give away the location of the owner of the black tree that was the key to the barrier's anchors. Trinity couldn't blame him. She wasn't exactly great company. She had shifted from the bathroom to the couch on the second day where she lay curled in on herself and wallowing in self-pity.

Charlie came to check on her that day and she was forced to admit what had happened when he exclaimed in concern over her ashen clammy skin and the dark rings under her eyes. His guilty apologies only made her feel worse. Like it was her stupid body's fault that he felt bad, which it kind of was. He told her he'd change all the flours and clean all the bins out. She wished she could bring herself to tell him there was no point because she wasn't sure she'd be able to trust his food again anyway. She couldn't face the awkwardness. She felt tired just thinking about it. She felt tired of always being the difficult one. She felt tired of another friendship cut short that she never should have begun. She just felt tired. All the time. She curled back up on the couch and spent the afternoon with her eyes shut closing out the world, desperate to sleep but unable to.

Still on for tomorrow? Dante texted that night.

I got glutened pretty bad. Not feeling great.

You poor thing! Was it your landlord? Some people are so thoughtless. Let me make you feel better?

Trinity felt guilty again seeing her own unfair thoughts about Charlie fed back to her that way. *I'll see how I go,* she replied.

She couldn't sleep that night. She stared up at the stars

through the skylight with aching eyes, feeling trapped not just by the barrier but by her own body.

She woke late, almost lunchtime, feeling hungry for the first time since she was poisoned. Saifa was nowhere to be found. He must have left on a scouting trip again. She toasted some bread and ate it dry, testing her stomach's reaction. Her body seemed to have finally stopped attacking itself. When she managed to keep down an instant coffee, she decided it was time to have a shower and venture out for some fresh air.

Another text came from Dante as she was getting dressed. *Are we on for tonight? Fern is desperate to see you.*

Trinity grinned at the photo of the cute huntaway with her tongue lolling out and tried to decide if she had the energy to interact with someone. Screw it. She deserved a night out. And if he really did have a wheat allergy it should be safe. *Yeah. See you at five,* she replied.

She swapped the everyday underwear she'd been putting on for something lacy and matching. As long as she was going out, she might as well feel pretty. It would make a nice change from feeling green. She spent the afternoon catching up on the work that had languished while she was incapacitated. Saifa hadn't reappeared by 4:30, so she left a note on the counter saying she'd be back late. After a brief hesitation, she wrote Dante's name and address down, just in case. Then she paused and looked down at the words. Had she ever mentioned Dante to Saifa? She frowned as she tried to think back on the last couple of weeks. Her thoughts clouded again like she was still sick and she struggled to focus. For years Saifa had been an almost constant companion, but he'd been away from her a lot searching for the key to the anchors. She hadn't even thought about needing to tell him about someone she met because he'd always just known.

The buzz of her phone interrupted her thoughts and she glanced down at the message: *See you soon, beautiful.*

She couldn't reach Saifa to talk to him now anyway. She could tell him when she got home. She paused again as she walked down the stairs. She had a vague sense she'd forgotten something important. Maybe she'd left the oven on? She shook her head at the ridiculous thought and carried on down the stairs. She felt better once she was moving.

There were two old women drinking coffee at one of the tables in the bistro as she was leaving. Charlie was cleaning down the espresso machine behind the counter. She hadn't seen him since he'd knocked on her door the other day.

"Hey! How are you feeling?" he called out as she tried to walk past with just a wave.

"A bit better, thanks."

"I feel so bad. Can I make it up to you? I could make you some soup for dinner. I promise I'll be extra careful."

Trinity could see the pained anxiety in his face. "No, thanks. I'm going out for dinner," she said, glad for the excuse.

"Maybe tomorrow night then?"

"I really don't want to risk it when I'm only just recovering," she said, and immediately regretted it. He looked like she'd struck him. "I'm sorry..."

"No. No. You don't have to be sorry. I understand. Enjoy your dinner," he said.

She hesitated at the hurt in his voice, but there was nothing more to be said. "Thanks. Hope you have a busy night."

The dizziness of the previous days had disappeared, but she still felt delicate so she decided to walk, rather than ride. She drew in a deep breath as she stepped outside and let the fresh cool air fill her lungs. That, and the last of the sun's warm rays on her face, gave her the energy boost she needed. She'd been laid out on the couch for too long. She was a creature of movement.

Even ambling at a far slower speed than usual, she was only ten minutes late reaching the imposing electric gate to Dante's compound. It opened as soon as she paused in front of it and she'd barely stepped inside when Fern came bounding up to try for an opportune face-lick. She laughed and backed her up.

"Down, girl," Dante said, grinning as he emerged from down the driveway. "Sorry about that. I told you she'd missed you."

Trinity crouched down to give her ears a good scratch. "I missed you, too, sweetheart," she said.

Dante patted Fern's side as he reached them, gently pushing her into a sit. He was wearing one of his trademark crisp white shirts again. His pendant hung free as he leaned down to pet the dog. There was something familiar about the obsidian shape, but she couldn't place it. She abandoned the thought as she noticed how scruffy she looked compared to him. A particularly annoying thought when he was crouched down in the gravel playing with a dog. She didn't need to impress him.

"Hi," Trinity said, standing up.

"Hey you," he replied, pulling her closer to kiss her.

Trinity was caught by surprise by the way her body vibrated at his closeness, but her self-preservation instincts were still functioning despite her body's unexpected response and the brain fog she couldn't quite seem to shake. She turned her head just enough so his kiss landed on her cheek instead of her lips and felt his hands clench a little too hard on her arms before he let go. She saw a quickly hidden flash of frustration cross his face.

He leaned forward again to kiss her other cheek, almost as if to prove he could, and then took her hand. "Come on. I bet you could use some comfort food."

Approaching the large mansion on foot, she got the full effect of the extravagant entrance that she had missed when they'd driven into the basement previously. A driveway lined with perfectly manicured topiary, black marble tile steps flanked by ionic columns that soared up two stories, and a double-width modernist front door in sharp contrast to the classical architecture that somehow pulled everything together. The way the driveway formed a roundabout at the entrance made her feel like she was in some sort of Jane Austen movie.

"How are you feeling today?" Dante asked, as their feet

crunched in the gravel and Fern weaved between them in excitement.

"Much better than I was."

"Excellent. Better enough to indulge me a little with dinner?"

He was watching her with those blue-grey eyes and a cheeky expression on his face but there was something else there that made her hesitate. It was partly that same loneliness she'd seen before but there was something else there as well, something almost hungry. She couldn't help but compare it to staring into Charlie's eyes. Charlie who'd been the only person close to her who wanted to feed her, take care of her, rather than devour her. What was she doing here? She frowned and started to pull her hand away, but then Dante smiled again. The hand that held hers was stroking her fingers gently and the light reflecting off his pendant caught her eyes. The soft geometric angles of the obsidian were fascinating and she could feel the soft pressure of his fingers drawing her anxiety away. Calm stole through her body and she smiled back at him. "What did you have in mind?"

"I thought we could dress up a little. For fun," he lifted her hand to his lips and kissed her fingers, waiting for her response.

Heat trickled down her arm from his lips and she felt like she'd stepped into a warm bath. Was that normal? She tried to chase that feeling she'd forgotten something important, but she was too relaxed. Relaxed was good right? She didn't get to relax very often, but still she hesitated. "I don't have anything else to wear, and you're already dressed up."

He turned her hand over and kissed the inside of her wrist this time. "I have something for you."

Adrenaline was a friendly buzz spreading from his touch, replacing the relaxation she'd been feeling with something else entirely. She felt like she was tearing down a single-track beyond her skill and the only way out was to keep going to the end and hope she didn't bail. She shook her head a little to dispel the feeling. It must be the lingering effects of the gluten. It always messed with how she experienced emotion.

"Are you going to go all rich-guy on me?"

"Just a little. It'll be fun," he said, tugging her hand to lead her into the house. She resisted a moment more, certain there was something she was supposed to remember, but the energy tingling through her blood seemed to be drawing her towards the house as much as Dante was.

The something turned out to be a little black Karen Walker slip dress. Its draping fabric felt like liquid as she pulled it on. Dante had left it in a gift box on the bed of a spare room he had shown her to. She looked over where she'd placed her phone on top of her neatly piled clothes and almost took the dress right back off again. Away from his intoxicating touch, it all seemed a bit much. She'd had enough making people feel bad for doing something nice, though. And it was a lovely dress. She wished Charlie could see it. Thinking of Charlie made her frown again. She shouldn't have come. Dante wanted something she wasn't going to give him.

The bedroom door creaked a little behind her and she swung around to see Dante leaning on the doorframe. His eyes traced down her body appreciatively.

"This is a little 'Pretty Woman'. I'll try not to take that as an insult," she said, her hands smoothing the fabric reflexively as she held Charlie's face in her mind in an effort to stop that incessant effervescent tingling she was feeling from sweeping away all her common sense.

He laughed. "Don't be silly. I promise I do not have a Julia Roberts complex."

Dante was stepping closer and she fought to make her brain work properly as her thoughts drifted away before she could catch them. "Why do I still feel… wrong?"

He took three steps closer, bridging the distance between them, and trailed a finger down her cheek. "You look beautiful. Powerful, even."

"Did you say something about having dinner?" she asked, too conscious of the bed behind her. She needed to get back into neutral territory.

"I did. Are you hungry?"

She shivered a little at the suggestion in his tone and then took firm control of her traitorous body to step away from him. What was with her, tonight? "Starving," she said, her voice coming out clipped and stern as she overcompensated for her failing self-control.

"Never let it be said that I stood between a starving woman and her meal." He gestured towards the dining room and placed one hand on the small of her back to lead her through. Even that small touch was distracting.

The room was dominated by a large polished wood banquet table, but there was another small round table set up in the bay window overlooking the garden. It was set with immaculate pressed linen, a tall tapered candle, and a triangular plastic shape. Trinity laughed as she approached and realised what it was. "Is that a gluten sensor?"

Dante smiled. "It is indeed. You don't have to take my word that the meal is safe. You can test every bite if you like."

"That's amazing. You're amazing," she said, turning to him to give him an impulsive hug. She'd never been able to check her own food was before. Now she could have a truly safe meal without her demon companion hovering nearby making sarcastic remarks. Wait. Saifa. Where was Saifa again? He should be here.

Dante's strong arms wrapped around her, pulling her body against his. His lips were on her neck and then her mouth and her thoughts were slipping away again. She was pressed so close to him that she could feel his pendant digging into her collarbone like a jolt of electricity. His hand slid down to the split in her dress and she placed her own on top, not really sure if she was trying to slow him down or not. She was beyond forming coherent thoughts.

"Dinner can wait, don't you think?" he whispered in her ear, the feel of his breath on her skin making her shiver again.

She hauled herself back from whatever cliff her brain was trying to throw her off. "Stop," she whispered.

Dante froze in place and then stroked a hand down her arm soothingly. "You don't really want to stop do you?"

His forehead was resting on hers and she could feel him trembling but he had stopped kissing her. That awful calm had started spreading through her again as his hand kept softly stroking down her arm like she was a cat she was trying to tame.

An image of Saifa as a Haast eagle spun in her mind. She focussed on the detail of each feather spread for flight. She imagined the air from his wings buffeting against her mind, driving away the incessant gentle pressure against it that was so insidious she hadn't noticed it was there. As her head cleared she pictured Charlie cooking in his kitchen and felt a stab of pure agonising guilt that drove away some of the haziness she'd been struggling with. She pushed away from Dante.

"I'm sorry. I didn't mean to give you the wrong idea. I think I should go."

Dante raised his hands as if in surrender. "At least stay for dinner. It would be a shame to let it go to waste." He turned away to pour two glasses of wine.

Trinity stared at his back and wished she could change down gears in her brain so it wasn't such hard work thinking. She took the glass of wine he offered on auto-pilot. The thought that came was like an air bubble struggling through a thick layer of oil. This wasn't normal. She tried to reach out with her power and felt nothing there. Even so, she would have sensed if Dante had any power, wouldn't she? Her eyes hitched on the pendant he wore and she closed her eyes against a wave of dizziness.

She felt his glass clink against hers, the ring of crystal on crystal only adding to the strange vibration in her head.

"To new friendships," he said, taking a sip of his wine.

She sipped her own to stall for time, not bothering to echo the toast. The dark red liquid was heavy in the glass. She watched the meniscus curving upwards, constrained by the clear crystal, just like Saifa was constrained. How had she forgotten that Saifa was trapped? Her eyes flicked up to Dante's.

"You look tired, sweetheart," he said, stepping closer.

She could feel her eyelids growing heavy. Her hand drooped and Dante caught her wineglass before it tipped its contents onto the rug. The last thing she felt was his arms wrapping around her as she sank towards the floor.

CHAPTER NINE

Trinity froze in place as she awoke in a strange bed. Her eyes blinked in the dark as her memory caught up to where she was. Nausea roiled in her stomach as she reached an arm out carefully to the other side of the sheets. Nothing, not even a patch of warmth. She was alone. She sighed in relief.

She sat up and fumbled beside her to find a bedside lamp. When she found it, the soft light stretched across an unfamiliar space, not the room she'd changed in but still a guest room. It had far more space than she was used to. Was that a couch by the far window? The bedroom was huge. She swung her feet off the side of the bed and looked down at the now rumpled black dress she was wearing. She wished she had the clothes she'd left in the other room when she got changed but they were nowhere to be seen, neither was her phone.

Her eyes hunted out the source of the ticking sound she

could hear and lit on a grandfather clock in a corner of the room. It was 11 p.m. She couldn't believe she'd fallen asleep. How embarrassing. Now that she thought about it, she almost felt hungover but she couldn't remember drinking anything. The last thing she remembered was changing into the dress. Had she eaten dinner? Her head ached, well not ached exactly so much as it buzzed. She felt a little like she was sleepwalking. She rubbed her hands over her face and tried to snap herself out of it. Saifa would tell her off for staying out so late when she hadn't been well. She winced as she thought of her demon friend. He'd be worried about her. She needed to get home.

The lights were on when she stepped out into the hallway. Dante must be around somewhere. She figured she was towards the back of the house because the hallway led through to the kitchen. There was still no sign of him. The only noise was the soft hum of the refrigerator. She opened what looked like the pantry door, vaguely thinking she'd see if there was something to eat before she carried on. She couldn't believe how hungry she was, how drained she felt. Maybe she hadn't had dinner then.

There wasn't a lot there. He was probably rich enough to get his meals delivered. There was just half a loaf of bread, a container of flour just like the ones Charlie used, and some condiments. She picked up the bread and almost grabbed a piece before she stopped confused by the twist-tie. It took her sluggish brain longer than it should to process that information—a twist-tie, it was gluten bread. That was weird. She didn't think anyone else lived here and he'd said he was allergic. Nausea surged inside her and turned to creeping dread.

She put the bread back and washed her hands by reflex in case there were crumbs on the packet. She splashed some of the water on her face, gasping at the shock of cold water on her overwarm skin. The white marble of the bench felt cool beneath her clutching fingers as she stared at the distorted reflection of her face in the polished steel of the sink. She strained to remember what had happened before she fell asleep. A sense of unease. Flashes of Saifa as an eagle and of Charlie. She held tight to them. When she tried to picture what Dante had said or done, her mind slid off the memories like they were as smooth as the marble she was leaning on. She felt a thought drifting out of reach and dragged it back to her: She needed to leave. Now.

Her bare feet padded silently on thick rugs as she rushed away from the kitchen. She didn't know where a light switch was for this hallway. First, she needed to find the front door and then she could go home and ask Saifa what was wrong. Saifa would know. She tried to reach out to him as she stumbled on. Usually, she could feel the connection between them even though she couldn't make herself heard. Now, she felt the connection slip away as if she had dislocated part of her mind. She whimpered at the stab of pain through her skull, launching into a careening run as if she could escape the hurt if she moved fast enough.

The walls blurred around her and by the time she halted her oblivious flight, she was well and truly disoriented. She must have turned down another corridor. She looked up and down the long walls covered in a mosaic of surrealist artworks half-hidden in shadow and tried to remember which ones she had already passed. A faint blue light pulsed at one end of the hallway and she headed towards it, drawn like a moth.

The room at the end of the corridor was an odd-shaped conservatory, comparatively small in the context of the mansion. It was the thin white joinery holding the glass that was generating the blue glow. The entire structure was separated from the house proper by about two paces. She could tell because the thick wool carpet, white walls and wood trim of the hallway gave way to an entrance enclosed in sheet metal for those two paces. The effect was like passing down a gangway and through an airlock. Even the floor of the conservatory was glass. She could just make out the rippling reflection of water beneath the space in the dim blue light.

As she stepped out into the ethereal space, she realised the room was triangular, a pyramid. In its centre was a circular table and on that circular table sat a shallow pot containing the gnarled jet-black miniature pōhutukawa tree that she had seen in her vision at the first anchor. She stepped closer in a daze, peripherally aware of the sloping walls of the pyramid that loomed inwards above her, concentrating everything that entered into that central space. She reached out a finger and brushed a black twig-like branch, sending the incongruous fruits that she had noticed in her vision swinging. Fruit did not belong on a pōhutukawa. She touched one, angling it into the reflective dim glow from the windows. It was a small obsidian black hexagonal disc, identical to the one Dante wore as a pendant around his neck. The buzzing of her brain had accelerated as soon as she touched the tree. Her thoughts shattered again as the waves of vibrations passed through her. She let the fruit fall, stumbling backward, and the buzz dropped to background noise again.

"There you are," Dante's voice came from behind her. "I was starting to worry I might have lost you."

She turned towards him and flinched in slow motion as he slipped an arm around her waist and kissed her cheek. Her limbs felt too heavy to move and when she tried to dredge up some magic to shove him away she felt only emptiness inside her where her visceral self-replicating power should be. "Where is it?" she whispered.

"It's dangerous letting it build up like that. You weren't using it, so I made a small release valve," he said, his fingers stroking the pendant around his neck.

"But Saifa needs it," she said, forgetting he shouldn't even know who Saifa was.

"You would trust a demon with that power? He is a predator. I'm protecting you, sweetheart. It's far safer to channel your power into a plant like this, a *natural* object. Do you want to spend your life being consumed by a demon?"

His words echoed her own despairing thoughts from the other day but they felt wrong. Trinity searched his face for the answers her foggy brain would not give her. She touched the pendant on his chest, recognising the tingling sensation of power-transference now that she was paying attention. She struggled to make her mind function, sending it along the minuscule trickle of power the stone was still drawing from her to try and sense what it was doing.

"It's feeding you," she said.

He reached up to brush a stray hair from her face, trailing his fingers down her cheek. "I have a life-threatening condition. The tree, the network, keeps me alive. It takes a lot of power to wind back death, and the roots to anchor me must run deep."

That didn't sound right. It didn't feel right. Her mind was still tumbling along the trickles of power the pendant was drawing from her. In her trance-like state, she let it carry her along, the threads of power twisting tighter around her as it travelled through the leaves of the jet-black plant like photosynthesis. She could feel the rest of the power that had been drained from her that night, and earlier, stored in the fruits that hung from the tree. Underneath that she could sense the residue of other powers. Hundreds of unique signatures.

"Who were they?"

"They were old. They didn't need that power anymore. They didn't miss it."

Her mind flicked back to the business card for the retirement home that Saifa had found and then to the portrait that hung above his fireplace in his lounge. "The old lady's precious gift," she whispered.

"She was the first. But you're different. It doesn't drain you. I don't need to wait by your deathbed. I can wait by your actual bed. And each day you will have more to give." His eyes had dropped to her lips.

Trinity wanted to vomit at the sickening words. Part of her mind was still drifting in the tree and she could feel the constant stream of power being sucked downwards from the fruit into the roots. The thread brightened exponentially as it split and was forced through an impossible number of narrowing root tendrils. When the power finally returned to the pendant that Dante wore, there were trillions of minute strands where once there had been a single thread. They found their way to his every cell, every telomere, reinforcing them against a dark tide that threatened to wash them away.

Dante's lips on hers shocked her back to herself. She bit down hard, tasting the metallic tang of his blood as he swore. His hands gripping her arms clenched tighter and the pain helped to dissipate some of the brain fog that the power he had drained from her had caused.

"Old age is not the kind of life-threatening condition that demands a cure," she said, her voice firmer than it had been.

"It is for me. And it can be for you, too," he said, pulling her away from the glass room.

She stumbled behind him as he strode down the hallway, turning corners until they came to a formal lounge where a fire roared in an open fireplace. He stopped by an armchair and turned to face her, softening his grip. She could see a half-drunk glass of whiskey on a side-table nearby. He must have been sitting there when she woke, celebrating his success at possessing her. His hand traced down her arm and lifted hers to his chest, touching her fingers to the obsidian stone at his throat. She tried to tug away as she felt the stone's power weaselling into her thoughts, fracturing and tainting them, but his grip was immovable. Saifa had been right. With the anchors and all the power stored in the key, he'd been able to hide every-thing from her. Not just his power, but her own thoughts. He'd been playing her from the first time they met.

"You are safe here now, Trinity. Don't you see? Your power cannot overwhelm you. I've lived so long alone. Just like you. We can be happy together. I know you've been happy with me." He kissed her fingertips.

She thought of her grandmother's warning that her relationships would consume her and gritted her teeth. In all the years of crappy men trying to possess her, the warning had never been quite so literal. "You're just like all the rest of them," she muttered.

"Who?" he asked.

"Men."

His laugh turned sharp. "I am like no man you have even known. Do you think I am anything like those string of no-hopers smashing in your windows hoping for one last chance with you? I did not chase you down. You came here because you were drawn here. Because deep down you want me."

Trinity frowned, desperately clinging to the thread of

conversation. There was something important there she needed to not miss. "How do you know about my windows?" she said, slowly.

Dante sighed and pulled her closer. "You are missing the point, sweetheart. You want me. You can have me. We can be happy." The words sounded like a chant, a spell. Because they were. Trinity shook her head, grasping at the shreds of her power that were drifting away from her for anything that would protect her.

"It was you that smashed the window at the bistro," she said.

Dante's fingers twitched where they held her and she thought she saw a hint of desperation in his eyes.

"And you swapped the flour to make me sick."

Dante growled low in his throat. "You were disturbing the anchors. You wouldn't want to hurt me, would you? We need the anchors so you can stay young, too. I love you. We can be happy. You don't have anyone else."

Her hands were balled into fists now. Her nails digging into her palms so the pain would help hold the power of his suggestion at bay. She did have someone else. Two someones. A demon who she loved and a bistro-owner who she wanted to find out if she could. "You said windows. My last flat. Did you make him break that window?"

Dante's eyes narrowed and he watched her warily. "I needed you closer to me. Say you love me. Say you'll stay with me."

His eyes were locked with hers and she couldn't look

away. His fingers gripped her chin so tightly, her teeth ached. His power wrapped around her, his power that was also her power, trying to mould her will to his. The urge to fall into his arms was overwhelming. She thought of the string of men since her Grandma died. Each had seemed perfectly normal, a boringly safe distraction from her lonely existence, until the day they snapped and did something like smash in her windows. Each time she'd fled further south, closer to Wellington, closer to him. Her relationships had consumed her, but not at all in the way she'd thought. It was all him. Distantly, she realised this would change everything she understood about her life, about herself, but she didn't have time to dwell on it.

She could barely skim enough of her own power to hold him at bay. But she didn't need magic to fight back. She jerked out of his grip and swung her knee up hard towards his groin. He cursed and twisted, taking the blow on his thigh muscle instead. She tried to run while he was distracted, but he'd grabbed her arm and twisted it up high behind her back before she'd taken two steps away from him.

His voice sounded broken when he spoke into her ear. "It didn't have to be like this. We could have had each other. Remember that. I don't need your consent to take your power. I just thought you might actually care."

He dragged her for real this time, her legs scrabbling against the floor as she tried to get free. The artworks from the hallway passed in a blur again and he stopped by a steel door within a few metres of the entrance to the conservatory room. He held his palm to the door and it swung open silently. She struggled as she realised she was heading to a locked cage and he slapped the side of her head. Not hard enough to knock her out, but hard enough to daze her while he snapped something cold and metal onto her wrist. Then he shoved her into the room and slammed the door shut behind her. Free of the influence he had been trying to exert on her to love him, she could finally scream her anger.

"Let me out, you bastard!" The words didn't even echo in the sound-proofed room.

The room was exactly seven and a half paces from wall to wall in each direction. There was a door in the back corner to an en-suite bathroom. There was a single bed bolted to the hardwood floor. And there was time. Seemingly endless without a window to break it up between day and night.

The cuff Dante had locked to her wrist was inset with another of the black obsidian fruits from the tree. It tingled constantly against her skin as it drained her magic as fast as she could produce it. Even without the fact that it left her helpless, it was a constant irritation like a mosquito next to her ear.

She hadn't eaten anything since the dry toast she'd had for breakfast the day before and her stomach was aching. She held her mouth under the tap in the bathroom gulping water to try and fill it. She wondered if he had video surveillance in the room. It seemed likely. But without her power she would probably never find it.

With nothing else to do, she sunk into memory, re-examining her life up to this point. Saifa had always scoffed at the suggestion she had a love-life autoimmune condition but she'd always had the evidence on her side to prove him wrong. Time after time, her relationships had self-destructed spectacularly and unexpectedly. But if it was all Dante's manipulation, maybe Saifa had been right and it was nothing to do with her after all.

Her Grandma had seemed so certain, but it wouldn't be the first time someone with foresight misinterpreted a vision. If she hadn't made those men violent, maybe she could let go of the guilt that had been a part of her identity for her entire adult life. Maybe she could let someone in. If only she wasn't going to be imprisoned here forever, she could go figure out what that meant.

She finally caved and had a shower sometime after that realisation. She'd been reluctant to take her clothes off if Dante was watching on camera, but it was worse that she could smell him on her skin after his manhandling of her. She turned the water as hard as it would go and let it drive away the memory of his touch. A skittering movement against her foot as the water started to cool made her scream in fear and she almost cried when Saifa's familiar voice filled her mind.

Do you know how long it takes to navigate a wastewater pipe in a body as small as a cockroach?

I... No. I can't say that I do. I've kind of lost track of time to be honest, she thought back to him.

Did you lose track of your mind too? Because keeping this guy a secret from me was phenomenally stupid, even for you. He might be powerful, but so are you. You could have fought it.

I deserve that.

Yes. You do, he said.

In my defence, he's been manipulating every man I met for years to get me here and you never noticed.

There was a long silence as Saifa processed that information. *Well, that explains a lot.*

So, how do we get out of here?

Honestly, I don't know. The barriers around this place are much stronger than what we were trying to break before. It took me long enough just to figure out the wastewater pipes were a weakness. I don't know how to break the door without your power, he said.

I guess we wait and see what happens then.

I guess so. I'd better stay hidden.

Thank you for coming.

I would never have left you, dear heart. We'll figure this out together. We'll get you out.

Trinity didn't say anything more as she dried herself off. She wrapped herself in the top sheet from the bed rather than put the dress Dante had given her back on. She couldn't bear to touch it. She forced herself to breathe deep. She wasn't sure she was going to get out, but Saifa wouldn't leave her alone. She could face whatever came with him by her side.

It must have been two days before Dante returned to the room. Meals had turned up once a day while she slept. Saifa had woken her the first time, but it had come through a hatch that was too small for her to squeeze through so there was no point trying to get out that way. An artificial knocking sound rang out from speakers hidden somewhere in the walls before he arrived.

After an extended pause, she realised he was actually waiting for a reply. "Come in, you sadistic bastard," she said.

"There's no need to be like that. It's not too late to change your mind," he said, standing framed in the doorway. He was holding her clothes in one hand. "I thought you might want these, unless you're attached to that sheet chic thing you have going."

Whatever we do, we need to do it while the door's open, Saifa's voice sounded in her mind.

Trinity snatched the clothes from Dante's hands and stomped into the bathroom to change. He was still standing in the doorway when she returned. She kept her distance and stood with her arms crossed glaring at him. The door was still ajar but he was taller and heavier than her. There was no way she could push past him.

"You had a visitor today," he said when the silence had stretched too long.

Trinity frowned in confusion. "What?"

"A lovely young man, impressive beard, a little dusty with flour."

Trinity froze where she stood, feeling like she'd bailed

and was careening headfirst towards a tree. "What did you do to him?"

"He's smarter than he looks, you know. He rang your phone while he was standing in the lobby and it was still in the spare room. I wonder what gave me away."

"What did you do to him?" she said again.

I can find him. I should be able to break him out if he's not in a room like this, Saifa said

Wait. Not yet, Trinity thought back to him, hoping she wouldn't regret delaying.

"That's the wrong question. The right question is: what will you do to keep him safe? I need you nice and compliant so you can send that demon of yours away when he gets hungry and comes knocking."

"Well, that ship sailed already. You tried forcing me to comply. It didn't work."

"No. But it would work if you let it, if you stopped fighting me. You would be free of this room. Your baker boy could go his way with a small memory adjustment. You would have a happy life. I swear. Once you give in, you wouldn't even know you were spelled. Your little demon will leave when he sees you are content and that you have nothing to feed him anymore. No more loneliness. No more running."

Trinity smirked. "I was only running because of you, asshole. And if you think Saifa will leave just because I ask him to, you don't know him at all."

She watched something in Dante snap as he realised she wasn't going to comply. His face twisted and became a mask of cold fury. "How many teeth did your baker friend have again? I hope I don't misplace any." He turned his back on her and swept towards the door.

"No, wait! Stop. Please," Trinity said, her mind frantically searching for options.

Dante turned back, smirking. "I thought you might see it that way."

"Let me think about it."

"No. Take it or leave it. Right now."

She stared at him. He was all about control. He always had been. She'd thought she controlled her movements, her life, and it had all been him. There was one thing she still controlled, though. Something she never should have controlled in the first place because he was family.

Saifa?

I'm here.

I release you from your oath.

What?

I release you from your oath.

She felt a rush of air as the bathroom door shattered. She had already closed her eyes against Saifa in the full glory of his true form, but she could still feel the absence that was his presence leeching the power from the air around them. Dante's scream had barely begun when it was cut short by the demon latching onto his face, siphoning all his power from him. Trinity could feel the pressure growing as Saifa swelled with energy, taking not just Dante's power, but every drop of the power stored in the obsidian fruits of the tree so he couldn't draw from it. Her body was compressed hard against the wall, and distantly she heard her own voice scream in pain. She knew it was done when the cuff on her wrist clicked open, clattering to the ground as Dante lost the last of his power. Saifa disappeared and the vacuum of his departure lifted the horrendous pressure that had held her motionless.

Trinity collapsed to all fours, drawing in huge gasping breaths. When she could do more than breathe, she looked over to where Dante lay, a crumpled heap of robes. She crawled towards him warily, alert for any signs of danger. His hair was bleached white and his face was shrivelling as she watched. His eyes were wide with horror, all his power gone, however many lifetimes of stolen magic coming to an end. She reached out and pulled the obsidian pendant from around his neck, tucking it into her pocket. Then she fled the sounds of his rattling breaths.

She found Charlie in the spare room where she'd left her phone. He was unconscious and tied to the bed with no signs of physical injury. It took her ten minutes to untie him and shake him with her hands and the first tendrils of her returning power into a groggily awake enough state that she could half-carry him out of the room. She thought about calling an Uber, but it was easier to bundle him down to the basement and into the Jeep. His head lolled against the window as soon as she shut the door. As she walked around the car, Fern bounced up to her, tail wagging. Trinity smiled and reached down to scratch her ears. "I guess we'd better take you with us, eh girl?"

There was one more thing she needed to do. She pulled

the car up in front of the house and got out, leaving Charlie slumped asleep. She grabbed a large stone from the side of the driveway as she headed out onto the perfectly manicured lawn to circumnavigate the house. She paused by the glass pyramid that seemed to almost float above the earth. In the afternoon light, its blue glow was almost invisible.

The stone flew hard and true, flung with all the anger and despair that had built within her over the past days trapped in a windowless cage. The sound of shattering glass, for so long the violent catalyst of hastily packed bags and lonely road trips to "start afresh", was now a prelude to possibility. The chance to be still. The chance to have a home.

She stepped through the hole in the pyramid's walls and scooped up the jet-black pōhutukawa bonsai under one arm. As she walked back to the car, she could see the way the sunshine was absorbed by the plant creating a nimbus of absence like a second skin. It reminded her of Saifa. She wondered where he had disappeared to. She wondered if he would return now that he was not tied to her by his oath. Tears welled in her eyes at the thought he might have left without saying goodbye or, far worse, that the power had been too much for him and he was struggling somewhere alone. She swiped the wetness away. She didn't have time for tears yet.

IT TOOK some doing to come up with an explanation for Charlie about what had happened that didn't involve magic and didn't result in him calling the police. It helped that he had no memory of the events leading up to confronting Dante, courtesy of the spell that had knocked him out.

She had somehow managed to manoeuvre him up to the flat when they got back and he woke to full consciousness in her bed with Fern curled up next to him using his chest as a pillow.

"What happened? Trinity?" he called out, as he struggled upright.

"Right here. I'm fine," she called. She brought him a coffee and made him stay in bed to drink it as she perched beside him subtly testing with her power that he was really OK. There was no sign of Dante's taint in him.

"Who's this?" he said, petting the dog's head.

"This is Fern. She... she was my ex's. She's mine now."

"Your ex that made you disappear for days and knocked me out?"

"It's complicated," she said, avoiding meeting his eyes. They were so kind and concerned that she wasn't sure she would be able to keep deflecting if she looked into them.

"Doesn't seem that complicated to me. He's a psycho. He needs to be arrested."

"I don't do police, OK?"

"Do you have a criminal history I should know about?" he joked.

Her mind flashed to the bones of her attackers from the night of the fire years ago, the property she'd damaged to access the communications tower, the withered form of Dante's body twitching on the ground as she walked from the room and left him on the floor. "Hardly," she said, forcing a smile. "I've just done some things I'm not proud of. I don't want to relive that."

He reached out and squeezed her hand gently where it rested on the covers. "Well. When you feel ready to talk, I will be right there for you. Whatever you need."

Trinity nodded. "Thank you," she said in a soft voice, certain she didn't deserve his sympathy.

"I'm starving. Fancy another living room picnic?" he asked.

Trinity smiled for real. "I'd love one."

Settled on the bright picnic blanket on the floor with cheese and wine with Doctor Who re-runs playing on the television, Trinity realised she was no longer in the flight or fight mode she'd been in for... how long? Years really. She wished Charlie was into riding so they could have one of these picnics up on a wild hillside somewhere. Maybe he could take the Jeep up the four-wheel-drive tracks and she could meet him up there. She smiled imagining cronuts and coffee looking out at the wind turbines after a morning ride, or cheese and wine as the sun set. She probably shouldn't ride back downhill in the dark after a wine though. They'd have to go during the week when it wasn't so busy so they could have some privacy. The park was so busy on the weekends. The image of the packed car park sparked an idea in her mind and a grin spread across her face.

"Charlie! I've got it!"

"Got what?" he said, smiling at her excitement.

"I know how you can get more customers! We can provide gourmet picnics like this for mountain bikers in the park. Sunrise cronuts at Mākara Peak! You can't get a more immersive experience than that! I bet they'd start stopping by the bistro more as well."

He looked doubtful for a moment and then she saw the wheels of his mind start turning. "I don't ride, though."

"Leave that to me. There's the four-wheel-drive track to transport food and I can get talking in the car park, take cards to give out when I'm on the trails. I'll win them over," she said.

"You'd do that for me? You're not going to move on?" he was looking down at his hands as he asked, as if he couldn't bear to watch her face for the answer.

"I'm not going anywhere," she said firmly.

PREPARATIONS for the new business venture along with her normal work kept her distracted from wondering if Saifa was going to reappear. She'd tried using her power to locate him, but he didn't seem to be anywhere nearby and she didn't have a map of the other planes to search.

She had scrubbed the obsidian pendant until she was certain no trace of Dante remained and restrung it on a short brake cable choker that she wore constantly. With the connection to the key, she could control the flow of power from herself to the tree so that it took only the excess that was a danger to her. A long night of intricate spell work reset the network so that Saifa would no longer be trapped if he showed up again and she directed the spare magic stored in the fruit into maintaining a complex weave of power that would hide her presence, and the existence of the anchors, from any being within Karori's bounds.

Thyme Laud's gourmet picnics were an instant hit and the bistro filled with riders grabbing coffee on the way to the park, and lunch or dinner on the way home after.

Early one morning under a pink-tinged sky, two figures stood on the majestic swing bridge in the mountain bike park, and one knelt down on bended knee holding up a ring. Trinity paused on her ride up to the peak and watched them. A bark sounded from further up the trail and she smiled.

"I'm coming girl," she called to Fern's eager face.

When she reached the peak, Charlie was busy spreading a heavily weighted tablecloth on a fold-out table for two set up on the lookout platform. The wind was no more than a zephyr, allowing him to safely leave the sparkling wine glasses and plates of freshly baked bread and cronuts on the table for the riders who wouldn't be too far behind. She left Fern in the back of the Jeep so the dog didn't knock anything over in her excitement and went to help with the finishing touches.

Trinity set up a wireless speaker tucked out of the way by the platform while Charlie placed a small vase of flowers in the middle of the table with a tiny copper string of glittering fairy lights wrapped around the stems. They stood back to inspect their work and shared a smile. It was perfect.

When their clients approached along the ridgeline, Trinity set the music streaming at the lookout platform and they retreated out of sight to the Jeep to give them some privacy.

"Cronut?" Charlie asked, pulling out two paper bags.

"Always," Trinity smiled.

Charlie leaned into the back seat to reach for the thermos of coffee. Fern thought he was trying to play and leaped over from the boot to shove her head under his searching hand. He laughed at the dog's antics, trying to push her out of the way to get at their drinks.

A voice sounded in Trinity's mind as she watched the man and dog with amusement. *Would you kiss him already?*

She almost choked. *Saifa! Where have you been? I thought I'd lost you.*

I was unstable. I couldn't risk hurting you. And you don't need me anymore, anyway. If she didn't know better, she would think she heard a hint of vulnerability in his voice.

Don't be silly! Of course I still need you. Who else will tell me when I'm being stupid? If you still want to stay with me...

Always, he said.

She cracked the window open and his pūriri moth form fluttered down to nestle against her neck before settling on her jacket.

I thought you were giving up the moth thing when I got a life?

I am. Just as soon as you kiss him.

Trinity rolled her eyes and smoothed her jacket down so he had a better perch.

"Sit, Fern!" Charlie said, laughing. A moment later he re-emerged holding up a thermos and two china mugs. His eyes lit on the green moth resting on her jacket. "You haven't worn that brooch in ages. It's beautiful," he said, putting down the mugs to reach out and touch Saifa's wings.

He has very soft fingers...

Shut up, she thought back, and then those soft fingers reached up to brush her cheek.

He didn't push, didn't take. He just waited, patiently, a question in his eyes. She leaned forward and brushed her lips to his. They were even softer than his fingers. His hand slipped behind her neck and pulled her closer, deepening the kiss as her lips parted for him. And then a very excited dog shoved her head in between them and knocked the coffee mugs to the floor. They both collapsed laughing as they convinced Fern to return to the back seat.

Charlie retrieved the cups and poured their coffee after placing a cronut on a delicate china plate in her lap. He held his cronut up between them. "To beauty and new beginnings," he said. His deep brown eyes held hers and the sweetness of his expression stole her breath away.

She touched her cronut to his. "To new beginnings."

A NOTE FROM MELANIE

Hello! I hope you enjoyed *Against the Grain*. It was so much fun exploring the mountain bike trails with my kids while I was writing this story over COVID lockdown, and even more fun dreaming up a local bistro that would fulfil my cravings for gluten-free scones and cronuts.

If you liked *Against the Grain* please consider reviewing it on Amazon or Goodreads. Every review helps!

Want more witchy fiction? Keep reading for a list of all the Witchy Fiction books written by my friends and I here in New Zealand. If you'd like to find out more about us and our books, check out our website at:

http://witchyfiction.com/

Melanie Harding-Shaw is a speculative fiction writer, policy geek, and mother-of-three from Wellington, New Zealand. Her house is nestled near the Mākara Peak mountain bike park, and she can often be found jogging up the Salvation trail at Wrights Hill reserve. Her short fiction has appeared in a range of local and international publications and her debut short story collection *Alternate: A Collection of 37 Stories* is available from online retailers now. Melanie is part of the 40 percent of her household who has coeliac disease and she's been known to drive 30 minutes just for gluten-free dumplings and donuts. She'd prefer a cure to living gluten-freely ever after, but you take what you can get. Contaminate her toaster at your peril.

You can find Mel at: www.melaniehardingshaw.com/ or on Twitter as @MelHardingShaw.

Check out the full list of Witchy Fiction books below!

Succulents and Spells (Windflower One), by Andi C. Buchanan: Laurel Windflower is a witch from a family of magic workers - but her own life is going nowhere until Marigold Nightfield knocks on her door. Marigold is a scientist from a family of witches, and she's in search of monsters. What lies ahead could reveal all Laurel's short-comings to the woman she's trying to impress… or uncover the true nature of her power.

Hexes & Vexes, by Nova Blake: Small towns are full of gossip, and Mia is pretty sure that no one in her hometown of Okato has ever stopped talking about her. Cast off by her best friend, blamed for a local tragedy – Mia had no choice but to run away.
Now, ten years later, she's being dragged back.

Brand of Magic (Redferne Witches, Book One), by K M Jackways: Hazel Redferne is an empath witch but she's given up on magic. When her neighbour, Joel, needs her marketing expertise, Hazel jumps right in to help. But an attack on her powerful aunt means unlocking her psychic powers is the key to protecting the Redferne witches. Can Hazel let magic - and love - back in?

Witching with Dolphins, by Janna Ruth: Friends before magic (or boys) has always been Harper's prerogative. Her best friend Valerie is everything she is not: beautiful, confident, and the most powerful witch on Banks Peninsula. They might not see eye to eye on everything, yet, when a sinister scientist threatens their coven, Harper is willing to give up everything: the man they both love, her life, or even the little magic she has.

Holloway Witches, by Isa Pearl Ritchie: Ursula escapes to Holloway Road leaving her former life in tatters following a bad break-up. She's looking forward to a quiet respite in a cozy cottage with a lush garden and lots of bookshelves, but instead she can't shake the eerie feeling she's being followed…

Familiars and Foes, by Helen Vivienne Fletcher: Adeline yearns for family, but for years, the closest she's gotten is her assistance dog, Coco. When a frightening encounter with a ghost brings an old friend back into her life, it seems like Adeline's about to find the companionship she's been missing. But her crush might have to wait. As the ghost's smoky presence increases, Adeline feels its hold on those around her tightening dangerously.

Overdues and Occultism, by Jamie Sands: That Basil is a librarian comes as no surprise to his Mt Eden community. That he's a witch? Yeah. That might raise more than a few eyebrows. When Sebastian, a paranormal investigator filming a web series starts snooping around Basil's library, he stirs up more than just Basil's heart.

Riverwitch, by Rem Wigmore: Self-taught witch Ashley Robinson spends most of her time on community work and picking up litter. When something goes badly wrong with the Waikato River, Ash is determined to get to the bottom of it. If only Bryony Manu, the other witch in town, could put aside their arrogance to help.

Jingle Spells: A mysterious child is spotted swimming far from the beach. A woman searches for a ghost in a blacked out hospital. One witch introduces her lover to her family, while another takes care of a magicaholic baby dolphin in her boyfriend's absence. A young man bonds with his pet eel, and yarnbombers accidentally summon something otherworldly. Jingle Spells is a collection of fun, quirky, and witchily magical Christmas stories by seven Witchy Fiction authors.

A Gap in the Veil, by Sam Schenk: As a mechanic, Greg can fix just about anything—except his broken heart. When a visiting musician dials up the charm after a gig in town, Greg's life looks to be taking a turn for the better. His plans to keep things simple between them are complicated by the awakening of a spirit bent on corruption. Greg must make choices between appearing distant or bringing his new friend into the fight, all the while saving Wellington from a past it had almost forgotten.

Raven's Haven for Women of Magic, by Anna Kirtlan: Cassandra Frost has zero interest in fortune-telling or brewing foul-smelling things in cauldrons, and much prefers the company of non-magical folk. She does her best to keep her powers under wraps to protect the secrecy of the Wellington witching community. But that's easier said than done when your grandmother lives in Raven's Haven for Women of Magic. Magical fireworks, mobility broom races and irresponsible use of cat litter spells are all part of the game for the witching retirement village residents. When Cassandra's forced to cast a spell in the open to save Adrian, a geeky graphic designer with secrets of his own, her two worlds spectacularly collide, and she learns the Haven is much more than meets the eye.

Alt-ernate: A Collection of 37 Stories: Melanie's debut collection of short stories explores alternate realities, presents, and futures through science fiction, fantasy and horror.

CENSORED CITY NOVELETTE SERIES

A post-analog world on the tipping point of Orwellian dystopia and the women whose choices will determine which way it falls.

***Would She Be Gone* (Censored City, Book 1):** When the State steals your words, you still have your voice. When they steal your family, will you have the strength to use it? Detective Virginia Wright is undercover in the criminal world of spoken poetry hunting suppliers of illegal open-access e-readers.

***Compact of Fire* (Censored City, Book 2):** Some words are hard to forgive. Some men are hard to control. Some mistakes can't be undone. Political aide Serafina Walker has been in damage control for the Secretary of Literary Safety ever since the actions of a rogue cop sparked a protest movement against state restrictions.

***Hell is Empty* (Censored City, Book 3):** When truth is made by those in power, even exposing the lies might not be enough. Journalist Deanna Myers has been chasing the censorship debacle right from the start and she's closing in, if only someone would run the story!

WHILE YOU'RE HERE...

Mākara Peak Mountain Bike Park was established by Wellington City Council in 1988, and encompasses Mākara Peak which dominates the skyline at the south end of Karori. The park is developed by a partnership between Wellington City Council and The Mākara Peak Mountain Bike Park Supporters Incorporated (a charity). Thousands of volunteers have donated their time to help build over 40kms of trails, planted tens of thousands of native plants, established a comprehensive trapping network to eradicate pest species and to encourage the return of native bird life. You can donate to support their work here: https://givealittle.co.nz/org/makarapeak